Living Will

Paul Edwin Holl, Esq.

Copyright © 2015 by Paul Edwin Holl, Esq.

All rights reserved. No part of this publication may be reproduced, stored in a retrieval system or transmitted, in any form, or by any means, electronic, mechanical, recorded, photocopied, or otherwise, without the prior permission of the copyright owner, except by a reviewer who may quote brief passages in a review.

This novel is a work of fiction. All of the characters, events and places are products of the author's imagination and in no way are intended to represent real-life incidents. Where the author uses the names of public places, personalities, celebrities or public events, they are used only to dramatize and to establish a time frame and point of reference. The story is not intended to depict any true situations.

To order additional copies of this book, go to:
Website: paulholl@wordpress.com

1-215-527-5635

ISBN 978-0-9916432-0-2

Printed in the United States of America

To my late father, Senator Ed, a man of many talents.

CHAPTER ONE

Southeastern Pennsylvania

After five in the afternoon, trains from Philadelphia rule the Borough of North Wales, Pennsylvania for an hour. Main Street traffic begins to parade in concert with the tingling bells and flashing lights at the crossing. Herds of suits with briefcases bump their way onto the wooden platform of the tiny station and disperse into quiet neighborhoods. On muggy afternoons, hundred-year-old oaks and maples provide a leafy awning for the weary commuters hustling below to the porches of their Tudors and Cape Cods.

It was on such an afternoon in the same town that William Hoyle pondered certain questions as he pushed his invalid boss in his wheelchair - *Doesn't everyone want to know what happens when they die? Is there an out-of-body experience or a light in a tunnel?*

The once brilliant attorney had gone beyond the threshold

of death. The eighty-six-year-old heart had stopped beating and his brain had flat-lined. He had dwelt in the period after death for more than an hour, the doctor had said.

So why is the geezer still breathing? The law clerk queried as he rolled his father's law partner, Chester Hoover, down the ramp from his father's office building, searching for self-control. *First I had to pick up all of my grandfather's work and now Chet's. I don't have time for babysitting too. I really don't have time for this burden anymore.*

Will knew why Chester Hoover was still alive. After the stroke a resuscitation specialist had brought him back snatching old Chet right from the grip of the grim reaper, right out of the jaws of death and asked him how it was. *Imagine that. The doctor actually thought that Chester might be able to describe what it had been like to die. The senile old fart would have been lucky if he had remembered his name. He's been senile for two years and I'm sick and tired of putting up with him.*

Three summers and every holiday break while in law school, William lived at home and worked with Chester Hoover reviewing wills, trusts, powers of attorney, and living wills. Chet, a nickname his boss hated, had written most of them forty-plus years earlier. His clients were dead, dying, ill, or senile like him. After graduation, Will continued serving as a clerk and couldn't become a licensed attorney until he passed the Pennsylvania Bar Examination. Nevertheless, he was doing the work of a lawyer as he had been for nearly two years while in law school.

Will had to use all of the strength of his six-foot frame to lift

Chester onto the passenger's seat and Evelyn, the old lawyer's secretary, as usual, thanked him for helping. Will liked Evelyn, right down to the reading glasses dangling around her neck on a chain. *That chain; so comical to recall how she would scurry about the office in search of her specs before Chet had bought it for her.* He had once felt compassion and pity for Chester Hoover, but those feelings changed to ones of disgust and resentment as his old boss failed to show signs of recovery and Will's responsibilities began to overwhelm him. Evelyn asked, "You didn't bargain for this, did you Will?"

What he had bargained for was three years of law-clerking in exchange for a partnership after Hoover retired: a sweet transitional deal that promised a very high income to a very young man who had a four hundred thousand dollar loan to pay off. This was not a college loan, like his friend Wayne's, but a "loan" from his father's Attorney General Campaign Fund. He had been dipping into the contributors' donations for more than a year to fund his weekends at the blackjack table.

"It's okay, Evelyn; I can keep things together. I know the work and the clients." Will waved to them as they drove away in Evelyn's Chevy sedan. Evelyn was a more valuable asset to the firm than anyone had offered to recognize, and Will knew it. She was always there to lend support. In fact, Will had rewritten most of the documents recently prepared by Hoover using Evelyn's computer that she graciously made available. Evelyn had been smart enough to realize when the firm had begun a downward spiral.

Originally, the name on the shingle in front of the building read "Hoyle and Hoover" referring to the late Winston Hoyle II, Will's grandfather, and Chester. Later it had become "Hoyle, Hoover and Hoyle" after Will's dad, Winston III, joined the firm. Will's father left the firm shortly after Will began clerking, having been elected as Pennsylvania's attorney general. That was just about the time that old Chet started leaving his fly open. It was clear that Will's youthful influence was sorely needed and Evelyn was more than happy to help him succeed. She knew that the future of the firm depended upon it. The next day, the Friday of Memorial Day weekend, he'd have the office all to himself to dig into the files and make changes.

The old people wouldn't be easy to deal with and Will lamented having to confront the firm's client, Lydia Dunbar, whose case was first on his docket the next day. He had remembered her from the previous December's break. Pushing ninety, the wealthy widow had been a chain smoker all of her adult life. A heavy drinker too, people said, as she remained at home cuddling the company books. *Life is ironic. There was Ruben Dunbar, the jovial, well-liked successful car dealer, married to the witch from the movie* Hansel and Gretel *and no kids to love. Ruben, who never smoked, died at the age of sixty-eight.* Will thought again about how much he was going to hate meeting with Ruben's crabby wife, but it had to be done and as soon as possible.

Will Hoyle had decided to spend the night in Chet's office, now his, just before the desk phone rang. *Oh dammit, I hope it isn't that crazy Dunbar witch again.* Will pressed the speaker button and said, "Hello."

A jubilant voice responded.

"Hi Son, and an early happy Memorial Day to you. How are you holding up?"

"Just great, Dad; how about you? Very glad to hear your voice."

"Thanks, Will; me too. Say, I have some exciting news. I can't elaborate over the phone, but in a nutshell, I've decided to run for governor of our great state of Pennsylvania. What do you think of that?

Holy shit! What do I think? "Gee, great, Dad." Will had been around politics all of his life and was keenly aware of the benefits it offered. He also had been exposed to the dark side; dealing with political bosses and demanding, large contributors to campaigns manipulating candidates with money.

"You don't seem too enthralled with the idea, Son."

Yeah, not enthralled at all with idea of being arrested for embezzlement after the campaign account gets audited. "Yes, I am. It's just that it comes as a shock so soon after you were re-elected to the Attorney General's Office."

"Well, in politics you need to strike while the iron is hot. We received such a big voting mandate that my advisers are telling me the time is ripe. More on that later when I see you. But now I need another favor."

"Sure. *What's one more alligator biting my ass going to matter?*

"I need a new treasurer for my campaign for governor. Chester can't do it anymore."

No kidding. He couldn't do it before his stroke either. How do you think I was able to get him to sign blank checks from the campaign account for me every Friday?

"Sure, Dad, my pleasure to help in any way." It had been that way for he and his father ever since his mother's sudden death at the hands of a driver high on coke; a complete dedication to the ever demanding profession of public service. Will resented the absence of a parent at his sporting events and camping trips with the Boy Scouts, but it was a resentment that he had never disclosed to anyone. Anyone knowing him during his youth had considered Will Hoyle the proud and happy only child of a prominent and successful family. Will accepted his father's thanks with the realization that he would soon be receiving campaign expense vouchers for payment, one after the other in rapid succession, for billboards, radio spots, TV, and public relations. He knew that now the campaign account, thanks to him, didn't have sufficient funds to pay such bills.

Will slept little throughout the night and awoke early Friday morning. He decided that it must have rained during the night. He watched a pool of water on Main Street begin to steam from the sun's rays as he pondered his fate. *Now I'm really up to my knees in crap. I don't want to be prosecuted for misappropriating the attorney general's campaign contributions and that campaign account has to now be rolled over into the account for governor. The press would be licking their chops over a story like that. And now, I have to replace all dough. Oh, God, what should I do?*

Washed and dressed in a white turtleneck, blue blazer

and jeans, Will descended the oak staircase to the law office lobby and fell into Evelyn's swivel chair. A touch of the space bar turned on her computer screen and he opened a folder called "The Dunbar Estate."

CHAPTER 2

The Borough of North Wales, Pennsylvania is what people refer to as "quaint" or charming and historic. Located just down the Sumneytown Pike from the William Penn Inn and the three hundred-year-old Quaker meetinghouse, it was a place for old money – in both senses of the term. Will went by foot on the brick sidewalks to Lydia Dunbar's three-story stone Tudor home. Friday had turned out to be warm and sunny with a whisper of a breeze, but it was little comfort to the young law clerk who was feeling depressed about confronting the widow Dunbar, among other things. He was certain that her situation hadn't improved - feeble and unable to walk or eat on her own - Will thought that he wasn't afraid of death as much as being in Lydia Dunbar's condition.

Pin oak trees lined both sides of the Dunbar driveway, blocking him from the sun, as he approached the house. Will removed his iPhone from his pocket and stealthily made his way into the shrubbery on its shady side.

His fingers trembled as he tapped the security code on

the pad of his cell. He had one saved message. "This is Lydia Dunbar calling William Hoyle. I must speak with you about stealing my money, you louse. You misused my power-of-attorney to take money from my account. How dare you! If I don't hear from you by Friday I'll call the police! You know my number."

Will wanted to listen to Lydia's voice once more. It made him angry enough to face her and to do something about her meddling. Crouching among purple azaleas, Will pocketed his phone with one hand while he cupped one ear against the stained-glass window of the widow's den. He listened for conversation coming from within. He could hear Lydia's nurse talking. His timing had been perfect.

Will waited impatiently, wondering when the nurse would finish.

"I'll just prepare your medicine before I go." She was about to continue when Will heard the widow's irritating, shaky sing song voice squawk, "Just get the hell out of here, or you won't have time to eat. Leave me in peace! It's not necessary to mash my pills in applesauce; I'm not a damned baby. Now go!"

The caregiver didn't respond and Will saw the den door swing open. He instinctively dropped to his knees and hid under a cluster of green shrubs. The nurse popped out of the house flipping a cell phone to her ear and a cigarette between her lips. Will could hear the rubber soles of her shoes squeak across the driveway to a mini-SUV. The car and its driver puffed balls of smoke as the vehicle whined down the driveway to Columbia Avenue.

My course in Elder Law didn't mention anything about a situation like this, Will told himself as he removed his loafers and inched open the den door. In contradiction to his prep school training, Will entered unexpectedly and without knocking.

The first thing to strike him wasn't a frying pan, as Will might have imagined had the old woman known he was coming, but instead the foulest of odors. The same smells had been forever sealed in his memory when he had sat by his dying grandfather's bed eight years earlier. *How do nurses get used to them?* To Will it was like breathing in a mixture of fumes from Ben Gay, Pine Sol, and urine. He felt the urge to vomit and might have left if he hadn't been shocked by the widow Dunbar's appearance. She had deteriorated dramatically since his last visit with her.

Sitting in her electric lounger, Lydia Dunbar was being attacked by dyskinesia caused by heavy dosages of various medications. Involuntary movements caused the frail woman to twist and turn in the chair as her face contorted. She struggled to maintain her posture as she sat holding two remotes: one for the TV and another for the power recliner. During their prior conversations Will had learned that for more than twenty years Lydia had been battling her persistent disease: an enemy within that would never cease attacking until every muscle in her body had been crippled. Then death would follow at an agonizingly slow pace.

For better or worse (and Will surely thought it was the latter), Lydia's powers of thinking and reasoning were strangely unaffected by the disease. She had once assured

Will, "Why, I could still balance the books of Dunbar Motors if I had to." The dealership had been in her husband's family for three generations before being sold for millions after Ruben's death.

A folding serving table stood next to Lydia's chair. It held one travel-sized packet of tissues and a half-filled plastic cup of what appeared to be water. Next to the box sat a small vial of tablets.

Will saw Lydia fumble with the chair's remote and raise herself to reach her medicine. Gulping hard, Lydia chased two capsules with water and began gasping for air. Will felt a rush of panic. *Holy shit, she's choking!* He began slapping her back but his blows failed to dislodge the pills. He thought about attempting CPR or calling "911" but a panic attack drove him to the door where he frantically wiggled back into his loafers and began running down the driveway, through the streets, and into the parking lot of his office building. *Oh my God, I screwed up big time this time.*

Will stepped over the door of his MG, fell into the driver's seat and called his pal, Wayne, who answered after two rings.

"Hey, buddy, I really need a serious escape. How about meeting me at Harrah's in A.C. to try our luck?"

A shocked Wayne Abercrombie, Will's former roommate at Villanova Law School, replied,

"Seriously? I can't believe you're even suggesting it after the bundle you blew the last time? What are you, made of money?"

CHAPTER 3

The Dry Tortuga Islands - Key West

She, the youngest woman to attempt the voyage as they had told her in Havana, wondered if the old saying was true, "To have nothing was to be totally free. Freedom is to have nothing to lose and to face your worst fears without hesitation. It makes you strong and successful."

As the nineteen year old gazed at the beautiful castle before her, she knew that it was true.

Ana Lucia Tejada was the only female on board the rickety skiff of thirteen refugees and had to stand in defiance among them. Even though she detested violence, the nineteen year old was forced to establish that she was not to be messed with during the first night. It had been the loud-mouthed one - the one with the torn cap and a fishhook in his right earlobe. He had backed off once he felt the sting of her blade slicing across his chest. The men then knew that this was not a woman to molest. Young, tall, slim and wearing a tight, black diving suit, Ana Lucia had quickly employed her skills as a spear fisher to send the men a message. *Don't even think about it.*

What she thought was an old, vacant castle sat upon an island. An easily swimmable stretch of water, looking dark as ink, was all that stood between her and freedom on a beach seventy miles from Key West. But she didn't know Key West from Ponce de Leon's Tortuga Isles. None of them did, and it didn't matter. They were in sight of land, and an American flag was waving in the night wind from a lighted pole on the beach. Then searchlights glared at them as sirens wailed to announce their unexpected arrival. Ancient cannons pointed at them and a moat surrounding all possible landing points discouraged their approach.

Only two inhabitants of Fort Jefferson National Park had remained to collect double-time for working the holiday weekend. Park Ranger, Jeffery Whippel, was jerked awake by the noise and by blows to his mattress from underneath his top bunk. Security guard Frankie Geyser kicked the mattress over his head and yelled, "Whippel! Wake up! Get out there and find out what the hell's going on. Take a shotgun and don't be afraid to use it."

At six-four, Jeffery Whippel was nearly a foot taller than Frankie and fifteen years younger, yet Jeffery was intimidated by the former Arizona highway patrolman even though his huge arms could have crushed Frankie's chubby ribcage. So the rookie park ranger merely replied, "Yes sir Sarge", as he popped from deep slumber under his Smokey the Bear hat. Fully dressed in khaki, Ranger Whippel slipped into his size thirteen boots and snagged a shotgun from the guardhouse gun rack. Sergeant Frankie Geyser held his rum-punched head to ease the throbbing as he looked out the window, over the Fort's wall, and into the pre-dawn mist rising from the tropical waters below. Light beams from the flood lamps, lost in the haze of the sea, revealed nothing to justify the howling of the sirens which brought back the memories that haunted him. For more than a year, since his resignation from the highway patrol, Frankie had been suffering from nightmares and flashbacks about his arrest for the sexual abuse of a Mexican woman whom he had caught sneaking across the border. Charges were never brought against Sargent Geyser but he was forced to resign causing him to develop an obsessive fear and hatred for authority.

Ana Lucia and the other refugees had just completed navigating more than fifty miles of treacherous waters to reach Key West, Florida, but they had mis-calculated. They hadn't been the first to do so. Fort Jefferson National Park and Museum, a former military fort and Civil War prison on the Dry Tortugas, became more visible as the sun pushed its mighty beacon over the horizon. Through a light drizzle, the aliens could see a bridge lowering over the Fort's moat and the shadowy image of a tall man in uniform, holding a firearm.

His Timberland boots sounded like bass drum beats as Ranger Whippel stomped across the tourist bridge over the moat and onto the beach. He held the shotgun in front of him in both hands, ready to shoulder it immediately, as he halted at ocean's edge. He spotted the skiff which had the lines of an elongated lifeguard boat and sat motionless, aground on a reef about fifty yards off shore. Black smoke from the boat's outboard spiraled skyward through the beams of the floodlights glowing in the mist. Ghost-like figures were crawling over the transom into the chilly water surging over the reef. Jeffery could hear the men cursing in Spanish as the jagged coral sliced their toes and feet.

As he watched, wondering what to do, two gunshots exploded behind his head. The young ranger fell to the sand grasping his ears. Frankie Geyser shouted, "Back in the boat!" He lowered the .45 automatic pistol from over his head and pointed it at the refugees. "I'll shoot anyone who tries to set foot on U.S. soil. Back in the boat!"

"I can't hear, Sarge" Jeffery said from his knees. "Do you want me to go to the boat?"

"No, dummy, I want those cube-heads to stay on the boat and paddle their way home to Uncle Fidel. If they get to shore we'll have to let them stay but if they don't we can have them sent back; just look at them squirm, ain't it great?" The sirens had ceased their sorrowful concert and the ringing in Jeffery's ears had begun to ease.

"But, Sarge, they risked their lives to come to freedom. Let's give them a chance to live their dreams."

"To hell with their shitty dreams. What about my dreams? We have too many of them here already sucking off the rest of us, cut the social worker crap and just do your job. Hand me your weapon, go inside the fort and call the Key West Coast Guard."

The rookie followed instructions and trotted back over the bridge, but he hated having to report them. *Why couldn't they have missed that reef and hit the island instead? I wish that I could pull them to shore myself. I'm not border patrol; I'm a park ranger.*

Frankie saw that there was sand in the barrel of the shotgun. Its barrel had jammed into the beach when Jeffery fell, rendering it useless: *useless, just like Whippel,* Frankie thought, but raised it above his head anyway, Apache style, and shot two more rounds into the air with his sidearm. The refugees all got the message and returned to their crippled craft. All except one.

"That's right, get back in your crappy boat you cowards." Frankie threw his head backward in laughter as he watched the Cubans struggling to climb aboard the skiff. Then his eyes narrowed and his face became drawn as he admonished them. "It's because of some dogs just like you that I'm here on this island instead of on patrol in Arizona. I'd like to shoot you all for that reason alone; just give me a reason."

Of the wet and weary travelers, one had slipped away from the floodlight beams into the darkness while Frankie was spouting words at the Cubans that they didn't understand. Silently breast stroking just inches above jagged coral, Ana Lucia Tejada glided parallel to the shoreline for about twenty-five yards, then turned and headed for the beach. Her real father's wetsuit clung snugly and kept her warm. Neither rain nor wind proved to be much of a hindrance and she was grateful for the rippling noise of the waves they created. Her father had taught her at an early age to dive and spearfish in the dangerous waters off Playa Grande so she had learned to fear neither the water nor the thieves on the beach waiting to rob them of their catch. Her father, an expert with the fishing knife, had taught her well. What the nineteen year old feared the most was being robbed of her freedom again.

CHAPTER 4

Fort Jefferson

Cracked and splintered shells, as sharp as shattered glass on a kitchen floor, dug into the teenager's palms as she crawled the final twenty feet to the beach. She felt her blood seeping between her fingers and it took her back to the day that changed everything for her; the day her father died in her mother's arms. The Dominican National Police told Ana Lucia that her father had been ambushed on his way home with the day's catch. There was nothing they could do when they found him on the road so they brought him home. His murderers were never identified.

She had to hide from the squatty *policia* holding the Cubans captive on the skiff. Over the edge and into the moat she slid, where prison sewage had been dumped one hundred and fifty years before.

The moat's wall was slick and provided little opportunity for her hands and feet to secure a solid grasp. As the young

Dominican swimmer clung to the side of the moat's wall, inching her fingers toward the drawbridge, she could hear banging and popping as Frankie Geyser emptied two more .45 rounds into the air. She could imagine her fellow defectors cowering in the boat and hoped for their safety.

Jeffery could feel the rain pelting his parka as he loped outside to Frankie.

"Where in hell have you been?" Frankie yelled. "I'm freezing my butt off out here!" Before Jeffery could answer Frankie yelled again. "Hey, where's my parka? Give me yours, you selfish loser, before I catch pneumonia. I'm in my forties and you're twenty something. I need it more than you."

"Golly, sorry Sarge, but I didn't know where yours was," Jeffery said apologetically as he slipped the garment over his head, "I'll stay here now if you want to go inside for a while, Sarge."

"Here, hold these," Geyser ordered as he handed the weapons to the park ranger and slipped on the parka, "Did you call the Guard?"

"Golly, yes sir Sarge, I sure did."

"Oh, so now you want to stand here like a hero to welcome the chopper and take all the credit!"

"Golly, no Sarge, I wouldn't" Frankie cut him off.

"Stop saying 'golly'! Who do you think you are anyway, Gomer Pyle?"

"Golly, gee no, Sarge."

"Shut up, Gomer, and get lost until I call you, understand?" Jeffery turned and began jogging through the sand toward the bridge.

Her hazel eyes peered from under a tight rubber hood, watching every move and listening to every word of the *policia* and she felt sorry for the tall handsome one for being so abused by the short fat one. The loud-mouthed one reminded her of her Cuban born stepfather who had taken her to his homeland and robbed her of her freedom. He too had been short and fat, with a loud voice and a nasty disposition - always drunk and smoking cigars. Lucy was grateful that the stepfather hadn't adopted her because she was proud of her Dominican heritage. *Will God forgive me for being happy when he died?* She prayed each night that he would.

Clinging to the top of the wall directly beneath the bridge, Ana Lucia, who had used the name Lucy after being dragged to Cuba, had heard their conversation. She couldn't understand all that the cops had said, but she could tell that the short one, Sarge, was mad as hell at the tall one, whose name was 'Gomer.' She had timed Gomer's gait from the beach to jump behind him as soon as he reached the bridge. Crouching and crab-walking in Jeffery's shadow, Lucy stalked the giant uniform right through the gates of Fort Jefferson National Park and Museum.

Once inside, the teenager fearlessly leaped onto Jeffery Whippel's back, clinging to his khaki shirt like a chimp on its mother, cheering "Mi free! Mi free! Mi free!" Lucy peeled the soaked rubber hood from her head.

At first, Jeffery didn't know what was happening. *Had the Cubans taken Sarge? Are they attacking me now?* Recalling his basic ranger training, Jeffery lunged forward from the waist to flip his attacker. When that wasn't successful, he raised his muscular frame with such force that he staggered backward. Lucy slid her wet suited body around Jeffery and ended up staring him in the eyes with her long legs locked around his waist and her slender arms latched around his thick neck. She hadn't cried in years but began sobbing uncontrollably as the fear and tension of her ordeal began to escape from within her. Her throat sucked short gasps of air as strands of her soaked, black hair slapped her heavy lips. Jeffery thought that he had never seen anyone more beautiful. He remained speechless as he continued to hold her while harboring an irrational fear - that her tears might wash the crystal blue/green color from her eyes that glowed before the rising sun.

A few more minutes passed before Lucy lassoed her emotions and began wiping her eyes with the back of her hands. It was then that Jeffery noticed bloodstains on her hands and feet. The bleeding had stopped but Jeffery decided that she shouldn't be walking until she was bandaged.

"*Lo siento* Señor Gomer *y gracious por todo.*"

"*De nada, mi linda.* Do you speak English?"

"Si. Yes, *pero* maybe a little Spanglish."

"You don't want to be seen by Sarge because he'll probably force you to return to the boat so you'll be sent back to Cuba. I must find a place for you to hide." Lucy tilted her head as if to be trying to understand what Jeffery was saying and felt touched by his concern for her but wary of his intentions.

Jeffery felt fortunate that all the inhabitants of Fort

Jefferson, with the exception of he and Sarge, had departed on the "Yankee Clipper" Friday night. He was certain that the six absentees wouldn't return until Tuesday to resume their respective duties. For his best friend, tourist guide Tilly Jewsel, the long weekend marked her first break from work in months. She had told him that she was meeting her politician boyfriend, at his beach house near Clearwater, for the long weekend. *Tilly's apartment will be vacant for two more days.*

Jeffery draped his slender visitor over his shoulder and slopped his way across the muddy campus to Tilly's cottage. His friend had confided in him that she had chosen that particular one because it was located the farthest on the grounds from Frankie's room in the guardhouse. At first Lucy struggled to escape his grasp but as Jeffery gently swung Lucy into a baby hold and tried Tilly's door he felt her body relax. It was locked and Lucy had fallen asleep in his arms. The rookie laid the brave young woman on a bench across from Tilly's door. As he was positioning his campaign hat under her head, Lucy's eyes slowly opened. Jeffery asked her, "What's your name? *Como se llama?*"

"*Mi nombre? Es* maybe Ana, *yo no se,* maybe Lucy."

"Golly, you don't know your real name? Poor girl, I'm going to call you Lucy. Okay?" He kissed her on the forehead. "Will you wait here? I need to find the key to my friend's door." Lucy nodded her agreement and offered him the sweetest smile he had ever seen. The big guy stood and ran back across the soggy quad to find Frankie's key ring. *It's in the guardhouse somewhere if it isn't on Sarge's belt.*

CHAPTER 5

North Wales, Pennsylvania

Early Tuesday morning Will returned to the office and bent to lift the newspapers from the landing. His pupils began to dilate as he glanced at one front-page headline. "Dunbar Matriarch Found Dead in Home: Police Investigating." Will's hands began to shake as he fumbled to unlock the door. He felt light-headed and sick to his stomach. Once inside, he sat on one of the leather-covered burgundy visitors' chairs in the lobby and lowered his head to his knees. *If the cops find out that I was the last one to see her alive I could be named as a person of interest; there goes my career.*

While playing at the casinos in Atlantic City, Will had worried about the possibility of police involvement. Now the old bitch was going to find a way to prevent him from getting his license to practice, dead or alive; even worse, he might be arrested! He thought about his options. *I could run. I could go to the police and explain what happened but it's too late for that.*

Burn the Dunbar house to destroy any evidence of my presence? No, too risky. But wait! They haven't contacted me. He looked through the window at the street. *No cop car, check the messages.*

Will dialed the code on Evelyn's desk phone and listened to the recorded message. "There are no messages in the mailbox." *Thank God!* He began to feel a little more calm - calm enough to read the entire article.

"Friday evening around nine, the North Wales dispatcher received an anonymous tip. The caller said that Lydia Dunbar, of the Dunbar Motors family, had died in her home. A patrolman arrived at the home within minutes of the call to find Mrs. Dunbar on the floor of her den. Police learned that a nurse from Senior Home Care Services had been in attendance earlier on Friday. The nurse was questioned and admitted having placed the anonymous call. The nurse also admitted having waited for hours before reporting the death, fearing that she would lose her job for having left the widow alone, permitting her to swallow large capsules. Over the weekend, the ME had determined the cause of death. The woman had choked while trying to swallow tranquilizer capsules whole. Police theorize that the nurse, in her haste to leave to have dinner with her boyfriend, left her patient to self-administer a medication negligently left sitting on her side table. Detective Hemmerlein, assigned to the investigation, might be asking the DA to consider filing criminal charges, possibly involuntary manslaughter. The investigation seeking justice for Lydia Dunbar continues."

No mention of Will. The law clerk sighed with relief. *They continue to seek justice for the old hag. Obviously, they didn't know her or they wouldn't bother.*

Justice. Will thought it strange that he hadn't recalled the term having been defined in his criminal law class - probably because it has many meanings: being acquitted of a crime you didn't commit, being executed for one you did, seeing the playground bully get punched, seeing the thief get his own car stolen, or becoming rich after a childhood of poverty. In Will's mind, justice simply meant giving people what they deserved. *Lydia Dunbar finally got what she deserved after being a witch for sixty years and the nurse, too. She had gambled with her patient's well-being and lost. Justice for them but where had justice been for Martha Kellner*

After scouring the office files for the firm's most elderly living clients, Will decided to make the Martha Kellner estate next on his list. A tragic story had been hibernating in the Kellner file for decades. As he read about Martha's early-married life, in a letter she had written to his grandfather, he recalled one of his grandfather's sayings, "No good deed goes unpunished." He had repeated it many times in situations similar to Martha Kellner's. Now senile and eighty-six years old, she had been a vivacious twenty-four-year-old teacher when she met her husband-to-be, Walter Kellner. He had been working as a mechanic at a small airport and aspired to become a pilot. A son was born on Walter's birthday one year later. Walter finally soloed when the boy turned eight. As a birthday surprise Martha had rented a two-seat Piper Cub for them to take their first flight together. The plane crashed and burned.

Martha lived alone after the accident for the rest of her life. Her grief, which everyone said had driven her daffy, hadn't been eased by the five hundred thousand dollar settlement she received. Decades of investment gains had given Martha an estate worth more than eight million dollars. Will was certain that the widow had little knowledge about or interest in her financial situation. *It's time to pay a visit to Martha Kellner. If only I had someone to live with her and gain her trust, I could get her to sign over everything. That would take care of the four hundred grand I need to repay the campaign account, in spades - before there's an audit.*

CHAPTER 6

The sound of a horn broke Will's concentration on the Kellner file. He glanced out the bay window to see Evelyn's car parked by the curb. Its passenger door was open and he could see a struggling Chester Hoover half way off the seat. His secretary appeared to be in a mild state of panic. Will rushed out to help. When he got to Chester, his helpless boss was nearly upside down his bowtie looking like a ribbon on his head. Chet's seersucker suit jacket was buttoned but his stomach still protruded below his vest. One polished brown wingtip was on the footrest of his wheelchair, but the other was still stuck inside the Chevy. The fleshy knuckles of his left hand were white from his stranglehold on the handle of the car's door. Will straightened the old man and lifted him into the wheelchair with Evelyn's assistance.

"I'll roll him up the ramp if you'll grab the tank from the trunk, Evelyn."

Once inside the offices of Hoyle, Hoover, and Hoyle they locked the wheels of Chester's chair, positioning it to face the window, and attached the oxygen tube. Evelyn scurried away to the bathroom giving Will the opportunity to talk to his boss. "Big day today, Chet?" it was a nickname that Chester despised. "Wanna go with me to see batty old Martha Kellner? Might be interesting. I think you're both living on the same planet."

Evelyn returned and sat at her desk. "Thanks for your help, Will. I'm not sure I could have handled him alone."

"My pleasure Evelyn. Anytime. I just wish that Mr. Hoover was able to tell me something about Martha Kellner."

"Martha?" Evelyn asked. "What do you want to know; it's one very sad story."

"Hey, I'm glad you know about her. I was checking her file and noticed that her documents could use updating. I read about the plane crash. She wrote some personal notes to grandpa before he died."

Evelyn grinned and said, "Let's just say that that's because they had a very personal relationship."

"Really?" *How awesome. I wonder if grandma knew?*

"Thanks, Evie, I think I'll visit her."

Will double-stepped the stairs up to Chester's office, dropped into the leather swivel chair, and opened Martha's file. Hoover had written her will and Will's grandfather was her executor, attorney-in-fact, and trustee. *Why, you sly old fox you. Way to go, GP.*

The heir to the firm printed some documents and was stuffing them into his briefcase when his intercom buzzed. "Yes, Evelyn?"

"Phone call. It's a detective Hemmerlein on the line about Lydia Dunbar. I guess you've heard about what happened to her."

"No" Will lied, "I haven't, what's he want with me?"

"I didn't ask. He just said that he was calling about the Dunbar investigation."

The word "investigation" caused Will to feel nervous again. "Okay. Tell him I'm on the other line and ask if he can hold." He needed time to think. *Why would he want to speak with me? What is there to connect me to Lydia? Did someone see me? Did I leave something in her house?*

Will picked up after a few minutes. The detective summarized the facts as reported in the newspaper that morning. He also mentioned that Lydia's nurse would most likely be formally charged that week, *so why was he calling?*

"Mrs. Dunbar's cell phone shows that she made a call to your office one week ago, last Tuesday. Did you speak with her?"

"No, detective, but she left a message."

"Did you return her call?"

"No, I didn't, because I knew what it was about and I didn't want to get involved."

"Please explain."

"I don't want to get anyone in trouble, but Lydia had complained before about her nurse. She said on many occasions that she had felt neglected. I told her to contact the home care agency and complain. I'm sure you understand that I felt I couldn't do much, legally, at that point."

"I see. So you didn't speak with Mrs. Dunbar after that call?"

"No."

"Where were you last Friday?"

"I went to the shore for the weekend."

"So you didn't talk to or visit with Mrs. Dunbar on Friday?"

"No." Will knew he had taken a gamble by lying, but what other choice had he?

"Okay, Mr. Hoyle, that's all for now. Thanks for taking my call."

Will thanked the detective and promised to help in any way that he could. The conversation ended with the law clerk feeling uneasy, but he had to forget about Lydia Dunbar. Martha Kellner was overdue for a visit from the firm.

CHAPTER 7

To ranger Whippel it felt like a mild earthquake and sounded like a scene from a war movie. The guardhouse vibrated and its windowpanes rattled from the gusts of air as the huge helicopter landed just outside the walls. Jeffery watched the giant orange and white bird slowly descend. Its rotor blades waved up and down, like the wings of an ancient albatross, as the chopper came to rest. Minutes before, the crew had hovered over the skiff, bull-horning directions in Spanish. They lowered life vests and instructed the refugees to remain on the boat until a Coast Guard cutter arrived to transport them to the Key West station. The park ranger could see Frankie Geyser running in the surf toward the aircraft yelling to the guardsmen, "I captured them single-handed!"

Jeffery couldn't risk taking time to search for the key to Tilly's cottage. He quickly rummaged through some drawers, without success, and then started back to Lucy. As he jogged across the museum's soggy quad he heard the great door squeak open. Jeffery envisioned Frankie escorting the chopper crew into Fort Jefferson. Looking ahead, he was shocked to see Lucy running toward him, waving, with something in her hand. He shouted, "*regresa, regresa!* Go back!"

Before she could understand what Gomer wanted her to do, they met. He grabbed Lucy's hand and together they jogged back to the apartment of Tilly, the tour guide. Jeffery pulled Lucy to the ground with him, and they crawled backward under the bench she had used. He prayed that Frankie hadn't seen them, while thinking about the consequences of that happening. *The guardsmen would probably arrest her if Frankie didn't open fire on them first.* Jeffery's fear of Sarge doing such a thing arose from Frankie's constant bragging about the dozens of undocumented, immigrant women and girls he had molested in Texas and New Mexico after leaving the police force. Jeffery felt certain that had Sarge seen Lucy he would hunt her and molest her also.

Fortunately, the security Guard and the chopper crew had been too busy talking to notice the two as they climbed the staircase to the guardhouse. Lucy held her hand in front of him, displaying a silver key between her fingers. Gomer asked, "Is that a key to the apartment door?" She nodded "yes." "But how?"

"Es there, in the *flores*," Lucy interjected, pointing to a flower pot on the floor next to the door. "Mi mama doing dis when she go out the *casa.*" *Golly,* he thought, *she's not only beautiful but smart too.*

Jeffery Whippel was surprised to find that Tilly Jewsel's apartment resembled a Black Friday clearance sale at Macy's.

It didn't seem to faze Lucy for a moment. She used the toilet, jumped in the shower, and was asleep in Lucy's double bed in less than twenty minutes. Jeffery watched her sleep as he repeatedly parted the window curtain, looking for activity from the guardhouse. No one was in sight, and Jeffery assumed that Frankie was content to have the guardsmen to himself, with the junior park ranger out of sight. He sat on the bed admiring her. He smelled her hair, held her hand, and kissed the cut marks. He gently touched the tan skin of her back above the white towel she had wrapped around her body. Jeffery searched Tilly's bathroom until he found a box of bandages. He returned to the sleeping Lucy and gently placed small patches over each cut he could find on her hands and feet. *I will do anything to protect you Lucy and everything possible to make you mine.*

He needed to keep park guard Frankie Geyser from discovering Lucy during his rounds until his friend, Tilly Jewsel, returned to resume her tour guide duties. *Tilly will know what to do. She is smart and has connections through that boyfriend of hers. I have to divert Sarge's attention. Keep him in the guardhouse as long as possible.* Jeffery wasn't sure whether it had been luck or a higher power that made the Coast Guard arrive just as he was able to find a place to hide Lucy, but now he knew he needed more than luck. He needed a plan and some help if he was going to succeed in keeping Sarge from discovering and probably raping Lucy.

Voices resonated in Jeffery's direction from the entrance of the fort. It sounded like there was a party going on. The sounds of the guardsmen's laughter made Jeffery sure that Sarge had treated them to more than just coffee. But the Coast Guard crew was now leaving and Sarge would be looking for him; he was not usually a happy drunk. Jeffery slipped away from the dreaming Lucy, locking the door and taking the key. He was sitting on the guardhouse step, banging the mud from his boots, when Geyser returned from saying goodbye to his guests. The guard was smiling from one tiny piglet ear to the other.

"Howdy, Jeffery my boy. Where have you been?" Sarge only called him by his first name when he was jubilant about something.

"I made your rounds for you, because I knew you were busy with those guardsmen."

"Thank you, Whippel. Let's go up and have a holiday drink. I have a lot to toast about." Jeffery thought of a plan. "Golly, Sarge, that's awful nice of you. Will you teach me how to mix drinks? I'll mix while you tell me what's making you so happy." *If I get Sarge drunk, he'll sleep all night.*

Frankie mixed the first drink: one shot of whiskey, some gin and rum, a splash of orange juice, some sugar, and a dash of Coke to top his version of a Long Island Iced Tea. Sarge sat on his bunk as Jeffery turned his back and made one without the booze. Sarge told the young ranger how famous he was about to become. The guardsmen were so impressed that he had captured the Cubans single-handedly that they promised to issue a press release for the Miami networks, and tell the governor too. Jeffery made two more drinks as the story dragged on. They ate lunchmeat from the fridge and Lil' Debbie cupcakes.

"I'll probably be on the news tonight," the guard crowed. "Hey! Go drag that skiff onto the beach for my photo-op." Jeffery stuffed the pockets of his cargo pants with food and left. Frankie spied on him through binoculars as Jeffery hurried back to Tilly's cottage with a sandwich and dessert for Lucy.

So you thought you'd pulled one over on me, huh? Frankie said to himself, *You'll pay for this, Whippel, and so will your sneaky little lover, Tilly. You're going to have to share Juicy Jewsel with old Sarge!* Frankie threw his head back in a hearty laugh at his pun as he pulled a mouthful of rum from the bottle.

CHAPTER 8

He couldn't believe his eyes. She looked like a Victoria's Secret model and he could feel himself blush as he looked away. With nothing to wear but her diving suit, Lucy had been compelled to squeeze into one of Tilly's petite mini-skirts and a tank shirt two sizes too small. Tilly's shoes fit almost perfectly, however, and Lucy couldn't resist trying on a pair of high heels for the first time. To Jeffery she was a red, white, and blue dream come true. To Lucy, Jeffery's sudden arrival caused her to feel self-conscious and she wrapped in the towel again and sat on the edge of Tilly's bed with a kitchen knife resting beside her.

Jeffery stood by the door, not knowing whether to stay or leave or what to say. The only thing that came to mind was the nourishment that he had smuggled for her. The park ranger reached into the large, flapped pockets of his cargo pants, pulled out the sandwich and held it out for her to see.

Tears began to well up, but she held them back. "You no mad at me for use the clothes of your friend?" She saw Jeffery shake his head indicating that he was not mad. Lucy couldn't believe how sweetly Gomer was treating her. She stood, checking that her towel was securely tucked, and began wobbling, in Tilly's high heels, toward Jeffery. Lucy nearly fell as she stumbled across the room causing Jeffery to meet her and grab her arm before she went to the floor. He held her and Lucy nestled her head against Jeffery's muscular chest. It was the first time since her real father's death that she felt safe and relaxed in the arms of a man and she had forgotten the knife.

The smell of Lucy's hair made him feel intoxicated and he wanted to stay with her, but it also reminded him that drunken Frankie was waiting. The park ranger explained that he couldn't stay, because he had some work to do. He mumbled about the skiff and Frankie. He also warned of the possible dangers should the security guard discover them. At the very least she would be returned to the others from the skiff and he would lose his job. At the worst, Sarge might attack her.

Lucy didn't understand. *What had she done wrong? Was her quest for freedom a crime? Isn't the United States the land of immigrants?*

He explained how asylum for Cubans required that they reach American soil and Frankie would probably do anything to deny her that privilege.

"But Gomer, I'm not Cuban, I'm Dominican."

"I think that makes it an even a worse situation for you which I will explain later." She wasn't to leave the cottage or turn on lights. She could watch TV only if she kept the volume low - very low. Jeffery asked her to just trust him for the time being. Lucy said that she wanted to trust him. He could feel his body tingle as they held hands before he left.

The wind and tide worked together to help Ranger Whippel drag the crippled skiff through the turquoise shallows. He lashed its bowline to a rusted anchor half buried in the beach and trotted in his soaked boots and pants back to the fort. Frankie Geyser was waiting for him.

As Jeffery sat on the steps of the guardhouse removing his boots, he could hear Sarge's blender whining for a rest. Two oversized glass tumblers waited on the counter. The ingredients for a Rum Runner cocktail and half a bottle of Parrot Bay swirled and foamed in the crushing ice.

"Hurry up, Whippel, I made us something special and I'm dying to try it."

Jeffery desperately wanted to return to Lucy, but knew that would be risky. He had to humor Sarge to keep him in the guardhouse as long as possible, so he responded.

"Be right there, Sarge, I'm soaking wet. You start without me."

The park guard grinned and replied, "No way, it's a holiday celebration!"

Reluctantly Jeffery climbed the stairs and entered.

"Here, Jeffery, toast to our fallen heroes wherever they may be." Jeffery swallowed. The concoction tasted strong but he had no way of really knowing. The only thing he had ever drunk before was beer — maybe twice. He could feel the effects almost immediately: a slowly growing feeling of euphoria, with each swallow tasting less strong. They toasted every hero Frankie mentioned: Washington, Grant, Roosevelt (both Franklin and Teddy), Eisenhower, Patton, Schwarzkopf and McCain. Then the ex-cop clicked Jeffery's glass to his other heroes: The Babe, Williams, and Lefty. Between each toast he'd replenished their drinks.

"I'm feeling lightheaded, Sarge," Jeffery confessed.

Good, *you sneaky dude; soon you'll feel high enough to get me some tour guide stuff.*

"Come on, Whippel, let's sit and talk as buddies for a while." Frankie sat on his bunk while Jeffery took their only padded chair.

"I know I'm tough on you sometimes, but it's only because I want you to be the best. Underneath we're real asshole buddies right?" Jeffery's brain was swimming; he didn't respond.

"Now, good pals tell each other everything. Right? Right. So let me tell you that I know you're playing with Tilly Jewsel. I call her Juicy Jewsel; get it?" Frankie laughed and slapped Jeffery on the knee.

"I know that she pretended to leave for the long weekend but hid out in her cottage waiting for you. I saw you sneak in to her place for a quickie this afternoon. But don't worry. I won't tell because she'd probably get fired if I did." Jeffery had been slow to comprehend Frankie's words. When he did he began to shake his head.

"Don't try to deny it, Whippel; I caught you red-handed through my binoculars. I have a clear view of Tilly's door. I watch her all the time and plan to jump her soon anyway."

"But no, Sarge, Tilly's not here."

"No? Well who was the food for? Her pet fish?"

Jeffery realized what a mistake he had made in answering Sarge and decided to remain silent.

"You don't need to cover for her, just as long as we're buddies. Pals share things. You share a little Juicy Jewsel with me, and mum's the word. Deal?" Jeffery couldn't believe what he was hearing, but couldn't think of anything to say. "No answer? I'll take that as a yes. Let's go see if Tilly is home." Jeffery watched the security guard strap his pistol belt around his stomach.

An early evening rain shower made them run across the campus and helped clear Jeffery's head a little. He concentrated as intensely as he could, planning what to do when they reached Tilly's apartment. As the two men stepped on the front walk of the cottage Jeffery began to speak loudly in Spanish, as a second language required for Tilly and all tour guides on the Dry Tortugas. Frankie became annoyed that he couldn't understand the conversation but Jeffery continued in Lucy's native tongue.

"The guard with the guns is here and he thinks that you are Tilly, the tour guide. Hide in the bathroom." She didn't answer, thinking that the guard could recognize Tilly's voice.

"Open the damned door, Whippel. Let's take a look." Frankie drew his sidearm.

Jeffery looked him in anger and said, "There's no need for weapons, Sarge; it's only Tilly."

"I'm security, shit head, and I'll decide that. Besides she might try to hit me with something. She doesn't like me and if she doesn't cooperate, I'll report you both. Now open it!"

Frankie burst in, expecting to confront Tilly with his deal, but the apartment appeared empty to him.

"I know she's here, Whippel; you were talking to her in Spanish. Where are you, Juicy Jewsel? Come out, come out, wherever you are."

"Sarge, I spoke to her but she didn't answer me, so I guess she went out."

"Out where, to play in the mud? No, no. She's here. Let's just have a look around." Frankie began searching as if he was still on a swat team. Squatting with his back to the bathroom door, gun extended, he turned the doorknob and shoved it open. The door banged against the bathtub as he entered. No Tilly.

CHAPTER 9

Her mail box seemed to be throwing up, and a mound of unclaimed newspapers bunkered the front door of Martha Kellner's Cape Cod home as Will attempted to reach its brass knocker. He hesitated before rapping, worried about the copper rain gutter dangling over his head that appeared to be the only support for a gang of slate shingles hanging on for their lives. On his way up the driveway he had glanced inside a Buick Century, slumped on four flat tires, and had noticed a family of rodents exercising squatters' rights. *Wow. This place is a regular five hundred thousand dollar fixer-upper.*

When his knock went unanswered, the law clerk was going to call it a day but then saw a curtain move from inside the bowed window of the dining room. He tapped on one dirty pane of glass and said, "Hello? Mrs. Kellner? Martha? Is that you?" He could see someone standing behind a drape. "It's me, Will Hoyle. You knew my grandfather, Winston."

Martha, wearing a pale blue cotton bathrobe, pressed her nose to the glass. Her voice was weak as she asked, "Winston?

Is it really you? I knew you'd come back to me. You look wonderful. Come around the back."

Holy shit, the old bat thinks I'm my grandfather. How could I disappoint such a cute little wrinkled face?

Martha Kellner was unlocking the kitchen storm door as Will rounded the corner of the house and entered the back yard. He saw her thin white hair fluttering in the afternoon breeze as she threw her head back and spread her arms as if waiting to be embraced by Leonardo on the bow of the *Titanic*.

"Oh my darling, you've finally come for your own true love," the petite old woman said as she hugged Will around the waist and nestled her head into his chest.

"You're even more handsome than I had remembered. We have a lot of lost time to make up, sweetheart."

Will thought Martha resembled a newly hatched chick in flight. "Yes, Martha, I've returned, and you don't look a day older either." They entered the kitchen. *Oh my God, it's the widow Dunbar's house all over again, but the odors are worse: different, stronger.* He saw a pot on the stove erupting like a tiny volcano and spewing coffee down the oven door. A brown puddle the size of a cow plop stained the linoleum. Martha cooed; "Hi Mitsy," as an orange cat with matted fur rubbed against Will's suit pants. The litter in Mitsy's box had been overwhelmed by her deposits, emitting horrid fumes that in his imagination he could actually see rising from the heap.

Will turned off the flame beneath the coffee pot and began opening the windows. Mitsy leaped to the screen over the sink to sunbathe as Martha continued to swoon at the sight of her young lover.

"Yes, Martha, we do have much catching up to do. Would you like to go to Hawaii?"

"Oh my! Yes, Winston. For our honeymoon."

"Perfect. I've prepared all the papers we'll need." Will removed the documents from the inside pocket of his suit jacket as he surveyed the dining room for space to spread them for her signature. "Martha, why are all these magazines piled all over your beautiful Chippendale table. Move some of them so we can use it."

"Yes my dear," Martha answered as she hastily began placing them on the chairs. She happily signed everything Will presented: the durable power of attorney, the living will, and her back-dated last will and testament, along with the self-proved will affidavit. The law clerk instantly became her attorney-in-fact, her health surrogate, and her executor. *Now I can help you from the bank to the grave, my sweet lady.*

"Thank you, Martha. Now, do you happen to have your latest financial statement? We should put our monies together. Who knows, after Hawaii we might decide to travel around the world."

The widow Kellner searched for it as Will opened the front door to retrieve her mail from the box and newspapers from the porch. He discovered Martha's quarterly report crumpled in the bottom of the mailbox.

As Will explained it to her, the new will was simple: gifts to charities, Trinity Church, the SPCA, and an animal shelter. Because her husband and only child were deceased, Martha would allow her executor to distribute the remainder of her estate according to his best judgment. *I'll have Evelyn notarize it all before she leaves the office. What time is it? Almost five. I might as well do it myself; it'll be simple enough, because she has the easiest signature to copy.*

Glancing at his new Rolex, Will said, "I'm going to run along now, Martha; gotta go back to work. How about if you straighten up the house a little? I think Mitsy wants her box cleaned; how about clearing off the dining table so we can eat later? I'll bring Chinese food for dinner. Meanwhile, don't speak with anyone about our plans. You know how jealous people can be." He looked back and watched Martha giggle like a schoolgirl as she threw him a whopper from her lips. Will breathed deeply as he walked to his red MGB roadster parked on the street. *I need to act quickly with this one.*

It was exactly five p.m. when he began wheeling Chester Hoover to the curb. As they walked, Evelyn inquired about Martha.

"Oh, she's just great: surprisingly spry and sharp as a tack. She studied her documents and asked a lot of questions. The only problem I noticed was her short-term memory loss. She forgot to turn the stove off, and the coffee pot boiled over. But other than that, she's seems to be doing well and talked about taking a vacation." Evelyn seemed pleased by the report and said, "Well, then I guess there's hope for us all."

Will returned to the office and keyed "China King" on his iPhone. He'd pick it up on the way to Oak Park.

Mitsy was still lounging on the kitchen windowsill catching the last of the sun's warm rays when he arrived. To his amazement, the only odor he detected was one of perfume. Candles adorned the dining table earlier dominated by magazines and paper debris. *Oh how love does move mountains and mounds of crap, too.*

Will set the table and they ate a romantic dinner, on Styrofoam and plastic, complete with fortune cookies. It later became a damp fifty degrees outside and Martha complained about the chill. Will closed the windows, with the exception of the one owned by Mitsy.

"Let's sit by the stove and brew some coffee, Martha; it'll warm us." They trashed their leftovers and moved to the kitchen, where Will found cooking brandy in a cabinet under the sink and turned on all four burners of the stove. They saluted with shots while the java stewed, and Martha's head nodded as Will tip toed to the door. He glanced over his shoulder to check that Martha hadn't awakened. Sweat ran down the inside of his shirt.

When Will left, Martha appeared to be asleep on the kitchen table and Mitsy appeared disinterested. *Aloha, Martha.*

CHAPTER 10

She sneaked up behind him on the dock of the bay where he sat gazing at the tall steeple across the lagoon that seemed to pierce the sky like a warrior's saber.

"Stick em' up, lawman, and give me all your love!" Tilly Jewsel stuck her pistol finger against Winner Hoyle's neck and gave him an upside-down kiss on the lips. She wore the knee-length hot pink dress purchased for the occasion.

"My gosh, Matilda, you look almost as beautiful as the flamingo we saw last night in Clearwater, at the Crab Claw."

"Almost? Well, then next time take a bird to dinner."

Winston Hoyle III twirled Tilly onto his lap. Behind them on his deck, a Latino couple dressed in white was setting a table for two with a candle lantern, crystal, wine, and all the trimmings. It had been their ritual for the last evening of each rare, long weekend they had shared in Winner's Madeira Beach Florida ranch home. Matilda Jewsel hadn't been the first woman to visit him there, but she was the youngest and, he hoped, the last. Pennsylvania's attorney general buttoned his pale blue dinner jacket and Tilly locked his arm as they walked to their "loving couple" meal of lobster, steak, and salad: "*surf and turf*," She thought.

After dinner and as if perfectly timed, Winner's iPhone chirped and Will's name appeared. Tilly sipped her favorite drink, Bailey's, while her man nursed a brandy. Father and son exchanged "happy Memorial Day" after which Will began his plea. Winner put him on speaker.

"Hey Dad, would it be okay if I fly with your pilot, Andy, this time to pick up you guys? I'd love to finally meet that woman of yours, and Andy told me he could use the company but that you have the final say."

"Well, since it sounds like you've already arranged it."

"Yes, yes, yes!" Tilly shouted.

"That's my answer. Thanks, Tilly." Will interjected.

"This smells like a conspiracy to me," Winner joked, "and I'll have to convene a grand jury in the morning." Will and Tilly had spoken by phone and through email during the year she and his dad had been seeing each other, but they had yet to meet.

All three laughed as they said their so-longs, and Will motored his MG to Wings Field in Blue Bell, Pennsylvania then climbed aboard the A.G.'s Cessna, ten-passenger private jet. It would be the third time in a year that the plane had retrieved its subject from his vacation house, but this time would be different. This time there would be an extra leg to the journey: Blue Bell to Saint Petersburg, to the Conch Republic, and back to Pennsylvania. Instead of booking Tilly a commercial flight to Key West, Winner had given instructions to change the flight plan. The jet was to wait on the tarmac of Conch Republic airport while Winner escorted his woman the rest of the way to Fort Jefferson.

Will, who loved flying and had taken five lessons during high school, sat in the cockpit with Andy while Winner and Tilly snuggled in the passenger compartment; it was her first time in a private plane. At the Key West Conch Republic airport she would experience another first. Their connection to the Dry Tortuga Islands would be by seaplane instead of the slower shuttle boat. Winner had a first coming also. It would be the first time he'd be returning to the place where they had met during a tour of Fort Jefferson slightly more than a year before.

It had all seemed so exciting and perfect to Tilly Jewsel until she recalled the mess she had left behind in her cottage. *I can't possibly let him see what a slob I am. It'll be dark by then, so maybe I can pretend the lights are out. It happens, you know; hurricanes, even tropical storms can cause that.*

Will and the pilot played blackjack in the government plane as the five-seat pontoon aircraft growled then took off, carrying Tilly and Winner over the mouth of the Gulf of Mexico on its seventy-mile jaunt. Tilly tried calling Jeffery on his cell.

When Jeffery's phone began chiming the national anthem, Frankie grabbed it from him and saw Tilly's name. "Ah, hah! She's looking for you, Whippel, but I'm not going to let you speak to her in Spanish again. No way! We'll just wait right here until she returns." Jeffery lunged at him, but Frankie backed away, saying "So help me, Whippel, I'll shoot you if you try that again."

"No!" a voice shouted from under huge pile of laundry on the floor, and something snagged Frankie's ankle. He screamed and his gun discharged as a pair of blue jeans moved below him while Jeffery latched on to Frankie's wrist. The two men wrestled and fell on Tilly's bed collapsing its mattress to the floor. The bullet had missed Lucy's leg by inches. She sprung to Jeffery's aid, but Frankie fought with surprising strength and she couldn't get hold of the security guard. The .45, semi-automatic handgun remained in Frankie's grip even though Jeffery had been banging Frankie's arm against the wall to dislodge it. It had discharged twice, harmlessly, during their struggle, and Lucy's thoughts became laced with fear.

She picked up Jeffery's phone from the bed. The display still held Tilly's number, so the Dominican texted the tour guide a message - *Emergencia!*

Lucy saw that both men were bleeding and realized that she had to take action to end the fight. She searched the kitchenette until she found a familiar tool - a filleting knife. Arms and hands flailed with legs entwined as she attempted to position herself for a stab at Geyser, but their rolling and tossing made it risky for her to strike. Just as Gomer was beginning to overtake the exhausted guard, Lucy saw Frankie's gun slip from his hand onto the mattress and his chest begin to heave. *Oh mi padre! He's having a heart attack!*

The security guard's body fell limp and his eyes began to

roll as he stared at the ceiling. Frankie sprang to administer CPA and Lucy pulled Tilly's bedspread up to Frankie's waist and went to the sink for water. Ranger Whippel had straddled Frankie and begun pressing on his chest when a two-fist blow to Jeffery's temples to stun him long enough for Geyser to wiggle away and retrieve his pistol from the bed.

Frankie pointed his gun at Lucy and Jeffery shoved her to the floor just as the park guard fired. Jeffery fell to the floor with Lucy and smothered her with his huge hands as he shouted curses at his assailant. Lucy wasn't sure how she was able to do it, but mustering every bit of her strength, she rolled Jeffery's heavy frame behind the footboard of Tilly's bed. Frankie' shot a round into the ceiling, screaming at the two. Once he realized that he had a clear shot at them, now trapped against the wall, Geyser stood over the couple entwined on the floor in front of him. "Now, if you don't want to go to jail *chica*, you'll crawl on over to me and make Uncle Frankie real happy."

Lucy flashed her piercing eyes at her Gomer, who squeezed her. She had closed her eyes, awaiting the worst, when she heard loud shouting and sounds of a scuffle. She looked Frankie's way, where she saw a tall man in a pale blue blazer strangling the park guard with his biceps and a petite woman holding Geyser's weapon.

CHAPTER 11

"Nice little place you have here, Matilda," Winner quipped, "and such friendly colleagues." The A.G. saw a big guy on the floor being tended to by a pretty young woman. The short, stubby one in his grasp was gasping obscenities that Winner hadn't heard since his Navy days.

Winner sat Frankie on the floor and stood guard over him; he tried to calm his raging antagonist while Tilly frantically scooped up her scattered wardrobe, which had ended in one big pile on the bed.

"I just want you to know, Winner, that my place was spotless when I left it. Just ask Jeffery."

"Which one is he?"

"The big one with the new hair crease. He's our ranger. The other one is Frankie Geyser, our security guard. Looks like a fight over the girl, huh?"

"Yes, and we better sort it all out quickly. I have two planes waiting for me, and your other co-workers will be returning in the morning. Right?"

"Yes. I'll talk to those two, and you cross-examine Mr. Tough Guy over there. Sound like a plan, Mr. Prosecutor?"

"I like it. How'd you like a job as my assistant? You'd have to be by my side at all times, giving me direction like that."

"Oh, I don't know, counselor. After all, it's pretty exciting around here, and you'd probably get tired of me being right all the time. Tough on the ego for an important dude like you."

Winner sat on a chair next to Frankie and replied, "I could get used to it. Try me."

"Not now, baby. I have a headache." They exchanged knowing smiles and began their inquiries.

"I'm Attorney General Winston Hoyle, Mr. Geyser. Jeffery over there sent us a message about an emergency as we were flying here. When we arrived you were standing over those two young people about to kill them. When I grabbed you from behind the bullet you fired went awry, fortunately for them and for you. I say for you, Mr. Geyser, because it spared you from being arrested for first-degree murder and possibly imprisoned for life. You should thank me for the good news. Now listen to the bad news. You can still be arrested for attempted murder, which could put you in prison for a very long time."

Frankie spat in Winner's face. "You think you're a big shot don't you? You don't know shit! She's an illegal alien and he's hiding her. That's a crime too!" Winner heard Frankie's voice quiver slightly as he spoke. "She must have jumped from the Cuban refugee boat, and then Whippel helped her. That's a crime; right Mr. Big Deal?"

Winner wiped his face with a garment from the floor and leaned closer. "Actually, Mr. Geyser, Cubans aren't deportable. The United States grants them asylum."

Tilly's Spanish needed polishing, but she had no problem conversing with Lucy. The tour guide listened in awe as the young, Hispanic beauty described her childhood in her beloved Dominican Republic and explained how she had been ushered away to Cuba by her mother and stepfather when she was thirteen. After her mother died she ran away and had been on her own for more than a year, spear fishing for a living. Then she met the criminal, Diablo, who arranged for her to escape in the skiff.

"After I swam from the boat to here, Gomer took care of me and saved my life. He let the bullet hit him instead of me. He is my hero forever." Tilly was about to ask why she called Jeffery Gomer when she was moved to tears. Winner went to her side. Keeping an eye on Frankie, he asked her to relate the story of the two young people.

Tilly did so and then asked Winner in a whisper, "Does it make a difference if Lucy wasn't adopted by her stepfather after she moved to Cuba from the Dominican Republic?"

"Yes, absolutely. That means that she's a D.R. citizen and not Cuban. We have to discuss this situation alone."

Tilly asked Jeffery, in Spanish, if he felt good enough to guard Frankie. When he said that he did, she handed him the pistol. "Don't let him move from there. Not even if he pisses himself." Gomer agreed, and she walked to the bathroom with Winner.

"Listen, sweetheart, if we turn Geyser over to the cops he'll blow the whistle on Jeffery and Lucy. Apparently she hopped off a Cuban refugee boat on which she was the only non-Cuban. She's Dominican, so she's here illegally with no status. Unless I.C.E. was to make an exception, that makes her a priority for arrest, imprisonment, and eventual deportation. Jeffery would be considered an aider and abettor for an undocumented immigrant. It's possible that Jeffery could lose his park ranger designation and his job. That, of course would be in the hands of the Department of the Interior. I remember my father always saying, 'No good deed goes unpunished.' This is a classic situation to which that slogan applies in spades."

"So what do we do, Winner?"

"I think that my little talk with Geyser made him scared about being indicted for attempted murder, and he doesn't know that Lucy isn't Cuban. We might be able to resolve this without causing all of us a heap of trouble. I'll have another talk with Mr. Geyser." After Winner returned to the security guard's side, they spoke quietly. After a few moments he addressed the group.

"Mr. Geyser has agreed to resign his position, in writing, and leave Fort Jefferson, never to return. Jeffery, you and Tilly will guard him through the night and escort him aboard the shuttle boat in the morning. The returning museum employees will be told that Mr. Geyser left to take a better position. I will request my counterpart in Florida to place Mr. Geyser on his law enforcement's 'watch list,' so he would be wise to leave the state. I have warned Mr. Geyser that having any further contact with Tilly, Jeffery, or Lucy would result in his arrest."

Geyser just listened and thought, *if I hadn't had that arrest in Arizona I'd tell them all to go to hell. But don't worry, I'll get even with you and the girl.*

"Lucy, I'd like you to agree to leave the island with me tonight for your safety until your immigrant status has been resolved. I'll ask my son, Will, to assume responsibility for you and resolve the legal issues. Jeffery, we need you and Tilly to hold down the fort. It was a selfless act risking your life for Lucy. You should get a medal for bravery."

Jeffery raised his bandaged forehead and said, "I don't want a medal, sir; I just want Lucy and I to be together."

Roaring and bumping through the turbulent night air, the seaplane trip seemed like an amusement ride to Lucy. Laughing and screeching with every tummy-tickling dip, she entertained Winner and the pilot all the way to Key West. Once aboard the Cessna jet Lucy kept Will spellbound as she told him the story of her young life and related her dangerous journey to The Dry Tortugas.

"You *comprende* mi Spanglish, Señor Will?"

The law clerk had understood enough to believe that Lucy was someone special. "Yes, I understand. You speak very well and you are brave." Then Will addressed his father.

"I have an idea I'd like to run by you, Dad. I'd like to have Lucy move in with our client, Martha Kellner. The old woman lives alone with her cat and could use some company. Her house is in Oak Park and very private. You can't even see the next home for all the trees. I think that Lucy would be safe there and out of the public's eye."

Winner waved his hand in front of his face and answered, "Will, she is in your hands. Do what you think is best for her while you're working on getting her a green card and an education. I'll pay whatever you need to accomplish these things for Lucy and hire an attorney for the office."

"Oh, don't worry about that, Dad; money is no object. The firm is doing great and doesn't need another lawyer. I'll be taking the bar exam in a couple of months and I'm going to ask Wayne to help me. You remember Wayne, my roommate at Nova; he's clerking in our Philly office."

"Yes, nice guy. I just don't want you to become overwhelmed, Will. You need time to relax and to prepare for the test. Please just let me know if you need additional help. One more thing: be careful not to cross the line and start practicing law without a license." When Will didn't respond, Winner went to the cockpit.

"Andy, would it be too much of an inconvenience for you and Margie to put Lucy up for tonight? That will give Will some time to arrange things for her tomorrow." The pilot agreed, the attorney general deplaned at the Pennsylvania capitol in Harrisburg, and the Cessna made its last leg back to Blue Bell.

CHAPTER 12

The next morning Will saw the red and blue strobe lights reflecting off the trees even before he wheeled his MG onto Park Avenue. As he crawled by in first gear, cop cars, an ambulance, and a fire truck obstructed his view of the stretcher being carried by the medics. *Oh what bad timing, Martha; I was just about to bring you a companion.* A man in a suit, holding a book, stood on the sidewalk in front of the widow Kellner's house.

Will observed Old Glory hanging outside every home as he rounded the block and parked one street over, watching the flashing lights disappear. *I'll wait until the party's over before venturing back to find out what happened to you, Martha. I guess we'll have to cancel our trip to Hawaii. Gee, what a bummer.* Only a few nosy neighbors and the man with the book remained in the area when Will braked in the driveway behind Martha's old Buick.

The suit had a white collar and held a Bible.

"Hello there, Pastor, I'm Will Hoyle, Mrs. Kellner's attorney;

and you are?"

"I am her minister, Reverend Hymon; Trinity Church," the white collar replied, showing off his best pulpit posture.

"Were you summoned to give Martha her last prayer?"

"Oh, heavens no, thanks be to God. I discovered her about an hour ago on her kitchen floor. This is my day for my monthly rounds to check on our shut-ins. Mrs. Kellner was alive when they took her to the ambulance, but the medic said that she had inhaled enough gas to have died. The burners on the stove were all on but not burning. Evidently, wind came through the kitchen window during the night and extinguished the flames while she slept at her table. Also, she had been drinking alcohol, based upon the smell of the glass in front of her."

Will thought, *you'll spread that all over the congregation, won't you Pastor?*

"Perhaps, Reverend, it would be best for you to keep your suppositions to yourself, for Martha's sake. It could be viewed as slanderous." Pastor Hymon bid farewell and took a hasty exit from the property. Will called Grandview Hospital, and learned that Martha had been admitted and placed on life support. His second call was to Lucy, at Andy's home, to inform her that he would be picking her up later in the day to take her to Martha's house. The third and final call was to his pal, Wayne Abercrombie, asking that he switch to the county office that morning. *Things seemed to be falling into place rather nicely.*

Chester Hoover, slumping forward in his wheelchair, had

been wheeled from his spot at the picture window before Wayne arrived at the county office of Hoyle, Hoover, and Hoyle for his first dose of "geezer law," as Will had referred to it. Will had convinced Evelyn that it would be better for his friend not to see Chester until he had been working there for a while.

"Good morning Evelyn, where can I find Mr. Wills and Estates this morning? He's expecting me." Evelyn directed Will's best friend upstairs and the lanky, former high school track star skipped up the narrow steps to the second floor.

"Hey, can you tell me where to find a good lawyer?" Wayne quipped as he got to the landing.

"Depends on how much money you have," Will said from his office as he motioned his colleague to sit across from his desk. They wasted little time in getting to work as Will explained their situation.

"At first it came as quite a shock when I realized that Chet was out of it, but I quickly realized how many of the clients I had become familiar with during my three years of clerking for him. I wasn't about to watch forty years of writing wills and trusts for peanuts go to another firm just when all the clients are kicking off. I did the math and I estimate that the estates in those cabinets are worth millions in attorney fees to any lawyer who probates them. For example, a five percent fee for settling a ten million dollar estate is five hundred thousand big ones. If the same firm serves as attorney and executor, that fee doubles."

"But isn't it a conflict of interest for an attorney to serve as both?" Wayne asked.

"Usually, but not for us. Chet was the preparer of the will, and in most instances the client's deceased spouse was named executor. I can handle most things through power-of-attorney, and if probate is needed I can do that work for Chet and be the executor too. There can't be a legal ethics issue if I'm not a lawyer yet and I run everything by Chet before I move ahead."

"Oh, so Mr. Hoover is still capable of overseeing things?"

"Yes, but I don't know for how long. So, we need to set things up before passing the bar in August. That's where you come in. We have hundreds of estate files that we have to filter through so we're working only on those where we have a sole survivor, living alone or in a nursing facility. The testator's executor needs to have died, and the testator must be close to death without many close relatives. Preferably our client has had no children. Now, do you have any ideas as to how we find those files?"

"Well, we know that women generally outlive men, so why not pull all the wills and trusts authored only by men. That should reduce the numbers quickly."

"Great! That's perfect, Wayne; that should work. All their names are on Evelyn's computer, and it tells you which clients wrote codicils after the deaths of their spouses."

"I'll get to that right now, Will."

"Good, but first let me tell you about a girl named Lucy."

As Will explained "The Lucy Assignment," as he called it, and his other challenges, Wayne became even more enthused for his new position as a law clerk.

"Let me get this straight, Will. So in about six months' time your boss became a vegetable, leaving only you to carry hundreds of clients on your back. You graduated from law school to find yourself inheriting a firm before you even have passed the bar exam. One client has died, another is critical, and you've been assigned responsibility for a beautiful woman who's also an illegal immigrant. Who said that practicing Wills and Estates is boring?"

"Grandview Hospital, good morning, how may I direct your call?"

"This is Mr. Hoyle from Hoyle, Hoover, and Hoyle. I'd like to speak with Mrs. Martha Kellner's attending physician."

"One moment please, Mr. Hoyle."

"Hello, Mr. Attorney General, this is Yasaman Fallah. I don't know if you remember me, but I was a volunteer for one of your campaigns. I'm Mrs. Kellner's nurse."

She thinks I'm my dad. Oh well. "Of course, Yasaman, you were a big help; thank you so very much. How is Mrs. Kellner, uh Martha, doing?"

"I'm sorry, but I'm not permitted to give information over the phone without authorization."

"Of course. As a lawyer, I understand, so let me do the talking and you can confirm or not. I'm assuming that she remains on life support. Is that correct?"

"Yes."

"Does that consist of full life support for all functions?"

"Yes."

"Okay, thank you. I will be faxing Martha's living will to the hospital in a few moments. Will you retrieve it personally and give it to Martha's attending physician? And can you tell me who that is?"

"Yes, I will do that, and her physician is Dr. Boston."

The conversation ended with Will thanking Yasaman again for her support and promising to fax the document immediately. He did so, and within an hour Will received a call from the eminent neurologist Dr. David Boston, who informed Will that he didn't like people trying to dictate their time of death by writing instructions in advance. "Playing God," he called it but he knew he had no choice.

That's right, doctor; it's the law.

CHAPTER 13

When he heard a sharp "clip-pity-clop" sound, Will looked up from his iPhone email to see Lucy wobbling down the front walk from Andy's colonial three story. His chin fell and gasped slightly as he stared at her body wiggling as she walked wearing Tilly's tiny clothes and heels. *Is that what she was wearing under the raincoat on the plane last night?*

Will vaulted out of his MG to open the passenger door. He watched her sit, then lift her long tan legs into the red roadster and toss her hair over the back of her seat. Her dark brown mane fell nearly to the floor as Will fitted her with a white Phillies baseball cap. The early morning had already become hot and humid, and as much as he was enjoying her appearance, Will decided that Lucy shouldn't be walking around town dressed like a teenybopper on the Ocean City Boardwalk.

Every man, woman, and child in the mall stared at them as Will led Lucy by the hand into Macy's with her dancing by his side. For an hour she tried on clothing: dress after dress, bikini after bikini, shorts and blouses. Whenever the salesperson walked away to wait on another customer, Will peeked into the dressing room hoping to get a glimpse of his beautiful charge. After another hour had passed with him enjoying watching her trying on shoe after shoe Will mused, *I never knew that I had a foot fetish.* Will ended the spree by piling everything on the checkout counter and paying cash. They motored onto Route 309 and stopped again to fill Will's trunk with food.

An eerie cry, a muffled howling sound, could be heard when they entered Martha's kitchen through a door in back of the house.

"Oh, *que linda*, mi pretty," Lucy sang as she lifted Mitsy from the tile floor, "You *es hambre. Como se dice*, Will? How you saying this?" She pointed inside her mouth with her index finger.

"Hungry. I think you mean that Mitsy wants food."

"Ah, *si comida*, food. She *es* called Mitsy?"

"Yes, and her food is here, under the sink in a bag." Will opened the door and lifted the sack to the middle of the floor where he scooped the nuggets into the cat's bowl as Mitsy wiggled in Lucy's hands.

The law clerk inspected the house thoroughly and felt satisfied that his charge would be okay living in it for a while. Will wasn't sure if Lucy liked the house, but he could see that she loved the cat.

Lucy wanted to know about Martha Kellner, and Will explained why she was in the hospital and not expected to live much longer. Lucy pleaded with Will to take her to visit

Martha before the woman whose home she occupied passed away. He would think about it, he told her, but had to leave to prepare for the busy day ahead of them. She was not to answer the door for anyone except him nor answer the telephone. He would return at two in the afternoon, when she should be wearing one of her new summer dresses and be ready to go visiting. "Open the windows to air the house and stay cooler," Will suggested as he moved about explaining through the use of physical gestures. As he left, Will took Lucy's hand, lifted it to his lips, and kissed it in royalty fashion. "You are fantastic, Lucy, and I've never met anyone as beautiful as you." For the first time, he noticed a shallow dimple appear in each cheek and he felt gratified that she understood what he had said. *It's just a matter of time before you're mine, you sexy baby.*

"What can we do?" A visibly irritated nurse Yasaman Fallah asked Dr. David Boston. "Why should a document determine when it's time for a person to die? How does the person writing it know what the circumstances will be? How do we know whether Mrs. Kellner would still want to end her life now that she's being kept alive?"

"Those are all good questions, nurse, and, furthermore, it causes an ethical problem for us as physicians. We must all take the Hippocratic Oath, making us swear to do everything possible to keep our patients alive." Dr. Boston spoke without emotion. "I have had to face this dilemma dozens of times before. In some cases the family states that they don't want the loved one to suffer, but what they really mean is that they want to inherit sooner rather than later."

"What relative to Mrs. Kellner is making this decision? No relative has visited her or called, according to her chart, during the first twenty-four hours. The only person we've heard from is her lawyer, Mr. Hoyle."

"Yes. I've spoken to him, and I'm afraid we'll have to comply with the terms of Mrs. Kellner's living will that he has faxed. Not only did Mrs. Kellner make the law firm her medical surrogate, but in addition the firm serves as her attorney-in-fact and executor. He faxed those documents as well. We will have to remove the patient from all forms of life support this afternoon."

Wayne proudly presented Will with a file folder as the latter plopped into the high-backed leather chair behind Chester Hoover's old desk.

"His name is Robert Shultz, a very rich retired jeweler living alone in the Rock Hill Mennonite Community. The guy once had five jewelry stores and made millions over a span of forty-five years." Will's pal had worked through the night digging through the firm's file cabinets in search of elderly widowed clients. Bob Shultz was the best prospect he had found so far.

"Terrific, Wayne. I'm sure glad you've joined me; looks as though it's paying off already. I'll call old Bob now to see if I can pay him a visit this afternoon. If he sounds likeable I might even take Lucy with me. One look at her should get his prostate throbbing."

"Hey. When do *I* get to meet this *chica* anyway?"

"Soon, but hands off for now. She's illegal, and I don't mean under eighteen."

The law clerks reviewed the files of other potentially lonely clients that Wayne had discovered and in two hours compiled a stack of more than twenty folders, which they spread upon the library conference table.

"There's gold in them there hills of paper, Tonto my friend. Reduce them to the top ten prospects while I go dig up diamonds with Bobby."

The handicapped ninety-two year old jeweler sounded enthusiastic to Will over the phone and said that he would be looking forward to meeting the grandson of his late friend. Will didn't disclose to Bob Shultz that he'd have Lucy with him. *I can't wait to see the expression on the geezer's face.*

Pink polka dots spun in a circle as she twirled the lace fringe of her new white summer smock in Martha's front yard while wearing her matching, pink flats. Will was once again awed by Lucy's actions and appearance. He just sat there in his car trying to describe her. *Glamorous in a child-like way; sexy but innocent; affectionate yet wise beyond her years.* Lucy waved and ran to him, about to explode with excitement, and he worried, *how will she come off to clients like Bob Shultz? Well, we are about to find out.*

"*Hola*, Will, we go to see Martha? Yes, *por favor*?" Lucy held a bouquet of Martha's yellow daffodils. "Her liking *flores* yes?"

CHAPTER 14

The shy, redheaded college girl was alone. Four fans circulated the humid air floating off the runways and through the windows of the small office. It was almost noon, and other than the mailman at ten o'clock, she hadn't seen another soul nor heard another sound apart from the humming of the fans. She had started to doze again, her head bowing to the Spitfire model suspended from the ceiling by a wire, just as the man in black burst through the door. The wooden screen door slammed as its spring jerked it back, and two-leather bound fists banged on the desk in front of her. The startled girl made a stage-worthy scream that caused the man to jump away from her as she stared at his knee-high black leather boots, hat, and gloves.

"Who are you?"

Frankie flashed a shiny badge and said,

"I'm investigating the kidnapping of a girl about your age. She was flown here last night against her will from Fort Jefferson, and I need to see your notes and flight plan for the next leg of her flight out of Key West." When the girl hesitated, Frankie said, "You would be obstructing justice by refusing to give me that information." She placed her palms on top of the thick red logbook resting in front of her.

"I'm not supposed to give that information to anyone."

"I'm not just anyone, honey; I'm a cop. Let me tell you what to do so I don't need to place you under arrest. You go to the little girls' room, and when you hear the front door close that will be me leaving. You can return and forget that I was ever here. *Unless I decide to come bang you in there.* Pretend you were dreaming so that I don't have to become your worst nightmare right here and now. Okay?" The coed hurried off, then Frankie spun the log his way and leafed to the last page of writing. *Bingo! Here it is: departure 10:35 pm, Cessna Citation, destination Wings Field, Blue Bell, Pennsylvania; a pilot and three passengers.*

Back inside his rented Chrysler Sebring, the ex-cop shed the sweaty uniform for a loose-fitting shirt printed with palm trees and a pair of bright green Bermuda shorts. With both the radio and the air conditioning blasting, Frankie drove from the private airport to the nearest Kinkos, where he placed an order for "business cards while you wait"; there he Googled, "State Attorney Generals of The United States." *There you are. Winston Hoyle III, Attorney General of Pennsylvania, Strawberry Square, State Capitol, Harrisburg, PA. Attorney at Law, wills and estates practice, Broad Street, North Wales, Pennsylvania. I'm going to even the score with you, Mr. Big Shot.*

An hour later, Frankie sat in his rental, proofreading one

of his new business cards. *Francis S. Holmes, private investigator, domestic, professional, and industrial services. "I keep an eye out for you"* Real catchy. You're a genius, Geyser.

Frankie programmed the GPS that spoke to him from the dashboard and then keyed Whippel's number on his cell phone, but the park ranger failed to answer. Frankie left him a message.

"Hey, Jeffery, it's your old pal, Sarge. I know you're mad at me, but I want to say I'm sorry for what happened in Tilly's apartment. I guess I was too drunk to know what I was doing, but I'm going to make it up to you. That's why I'm calling. I have some information for you about your girlfriend. Give me a call, and please don't let Tilly know that I called, or I won't be able to tell you what I found out. Talk to you later, buddy."

Frankie wheeled the Chrysler onto A1A and headed up the coast through the Florida Keys, North toward Miami. It wasn't until he had crossed the seven-mile bridge and made his way to Marathon that Jeffery returned his call. Sarge was sitting on the deck of the Buccaneer Restaurant, drinking a mojito and puffing on a cigar, when he saw the name Whippel appear on his cell.

"Hello there, Jeffery old friend. Thanks for calling back."

"Hi Sarge. Tilly says I'm not to talk to you anymore, but if you have information about Lucy I'd like to know."

"I do, Jeffery, but first, tell me if Tilly knows I called."

"No, Sarge, I haven't spoken to her today; she's been busy with tours."

"Good. Okay, here's what I know. Tilly's asshole boyfriend

changed planes in Key West and put Lucy on a Cessna Citation jet to a place called, Blue Bell, Pennsylvania. That's near where he lives and has his private office. I'm pretty sure that he's making Lucy shack up with him there but don't breathe a word of this until I can check it out."

"You don't need to check on her, Sarge, because Tilly will keep me informed."

"Come on now, Whippel! Do you really think that her boyfriend is going to tell Tilly the truth? Don't forget, he's a bullshitting lawyer. I'm a trained cop. I can tail them and report back to you without Lucy ever knowing I'm around. You do want to know what's happening to her, don't you?"

"Golly, yes, Sarge, but I don't know."

"Listen to me Jeffery. I'm the only one that can give you an objective report. You will never know for sure what's going on without that. I promise that I'll never even have to talk to Lucy, and she'll never know that I'm around unless you spill the beans. What do you say? How about giving me a chance to make it up to you? That's all I'm asking."

"*Hola*, Señora Martha, *mi nombre es* Lucy here in your country but in mi country *es* Anna Lucia. You a pretty woman and I like talk to you. I staying in you *casa* and taking the good care of Mitsy and you *flores*." Lucy continued talking non-stop, with her face close to Martha's, hoping that the dying woman could understand. All life support had been removed. "*Gracias por* let mi stay in you *casa*. I like this *casa mucho* and me taking for you some *flores*." Lucy held the daffodils directly under

Martha's nostrils to smell as she wrapped the eighty-six year old fingers around their stems. The hand tightened, and Martha's eyes popped open into a wide-eyed stare at her visitor. Lucy's cheeks puffed with happiness and her teeth gleamed as she asked,

"You can see mi Señora Martha, yes?" No response.

"You can hear mi Señora, yes?" Martha didn't reply and her eyelids fell together.

Lucy continued to talk, lapsing into Spanish from Spanglish, in the hope that Martha would wake up again. She spoke so fast that even she wasn't certain that her words made sense. Then she felt Will's hand on her shoulder.

"Lucy, relax and let Martha pass. It's her time," Will counseled.

"No! She like for living, not for the dying. She having the will to live, and you need telling El Doctor for helping her to live."

Nurse Yasaman Fallah had been standing in the doorway to Martha's ICU room the entire time that Will and Lucy had been visiting.

"Don't worry, folks. I'll contact him immediately to get the directive to reinstate life support." She turned and walked to the nurses' station before Will could utter a word, and Lucy kicked off her pink flats, sending him the signal that she was not ready to leave.

"Lucy," Will said reservedly, "we also need to visit Bob Shultz today, so we can't stay too much longer."

"You going for Señor Bob es okay, *pero* Señora Martha

needing mi." Lucy waited patiently, stroking Martha's hair and holding her hand until the medical team arrived, then she refused to leave the old woman's side while it worked to restore Martha's life support systems.

It was after five o'clock when Will finally ushered Lucy into the visitors' elevator. He called Robert Shultz and apologized for the hour; they decided to postpone the visit until Thursday afternoon. During the drive back to Martha's house, Will listened as Lucy talked with excitement in her voice about Martha's responses and assured Will that his client would recover now that she had been given a second chance on life support. Will thought. *Oh yeah, that would be just great! Especially when she sees me and asks when we're going to Hawaii.*

The law clerk and his assistant enjoyed a meal of salad, rice, and beans prepared by Lucy and served on the picnic table in Martha's back yard. They shared stories until the sound of thunder in the distance chased them into the house to close the windows and doors. Lucy washed and Will dried as they stood before the kitchen sink with Mitsy perched upon the windowsill. As they finished Will reached from behind her and around her waist to dry Lucy's hands. Her hair brushed his cheek. He kissed her head as he began massaging Lucy's fingers with the hand towel and pulled her back to his chest.

Lucy pulled away from him and reached to close Mitsy's window as the rain started. When she leaned forward, Will placed his hands on her hips. Lucy elbowed Will in the chest to break his grip and then moved to the other side of the kitchen and shouted, "I no like what you doing, Will, and I have the *amor por mi novio.* You no having *novia?*"

"*Novia?* What is this?" Lucy turned to face him and answered, "Es the *mujer.* The woman and *novio es* the man."

"So you have a boyfriend? A man in Cuba?"

"No, Gomer es here in United States, in Key West, and mi needing only he."

She must be talking about the Dry Tortugas where Dad found her.

CHAPTER 15

"Ashes to ashes, dust to dust," the preacher uttered over the urn standing on a table in the mahogany viewing room of Huff's funeral home.

Quite appropriate, Will thought, *After all, they do burn witches, don't they?*

Only Will and a handful of former employees of Dunbar Motors had been in attendance at Lydia Dunbar's early morning service on the first Thursday of June. Will had thought that the minister looked familiar, but it wasn't until they stood in the bright sunshine of the parking lot lined with hearses that he recognized him as the same Bible-toting Pastor he had met at Martha Kellner's home.

"Well Mr. Hoyle, it appears that death is following your client's around", Pastor Hymon said with a smug expression.

"Good morning, Pastor, and it appears that you have a corner of the market on death yourself," Will responded with an equally smug expression. "Have you visited Mrs. Kellner at Grandview?"

"Indeed I have, and just yesterday. Detective Hemmerlein was present too asking a lot of questions. He found it most curious that you are connected to both her and Mrs. Dunbar."

Will felt perspiration seeping into the collar of his dress shirt.

"Our firm just happens to have represented both families and has for many years."

"Yes, of course. That explains it. Please excuse me now, I have another service to prepare for, Mr. Hoyle." Will watched him as he slid into his black Ford Focus and drove away. *God, I hope that nosy cop doesn't go snooping around Martha's house.* The law clerk removed his suit jacket and tie, stepped into his red roadster, and sped off in the direction of Oak Park.

No patrol cars or unmarked Crown Victorias were in sight as he pulled his MGB into Martha's driveway. Her neglected Buick was still parked there, but its blue paint glistened in the sunlight. As he stood, Will felt cold water strike him, and he shielded his face with his forearms. Lucy appeared before him holding a garden hose, giggling and pointing at Will's wet pants. Will started to chase, but Lucy outran him, circling the house twice before he finally surrendered to a seat at the picnic table in the back yard.

"Wow, you've been a busy girl this morning. I see you've even been gardening."

"Si, mi liking the *flores mucho es muy bonita.*"

"Yes, they are beautiful and you can work more later, but now please get dressed. We need to go see my client Bob Shultz, the jeweler. He is in a retirement home." Will felt nervous, fearing that Detective Hemmerlein might show up at any moment, and he wanted Lucy off the property as soon as possible. "I'll wait downstairs and play with Mitsy." Lucy disappeared through the dining room as Will poured himself a cup of coffee from a sauce pan on the stove, ate a donut, and filled Mitsy's bowl with Meow Mix.

Her long hair swirled about her head as they sped along route 309. Lucy recognized the road as being the same one they had driven two days earlier to Grandview Hospital. She pleaded with Will to stop there first to visit Martha. At first, Will refused. *It would be stupid of me to agree; what if the old woman recognizes me and remembers me visiting? Worse yet, what if she can speak? No, not a chance!*

Lucy promised she wouldn't stay long and only wanted to see for herself how Martha was doing. She wanted Will to get a report from nurse Fallah. She wanted to give Martha more flowers from her garden, the ones that Lucy had told Will were meant for Bob Shultz. *Oh, but you are an intelligent one, sweet Lucia.* Will gave in, exiting at the blue sign with the capital "H."

Much to Will's relief, Martha Kellner was sleeping under medication when they arrived. Lucy placed the flowers on the bed stand and held Martha's hand while Will hurried to the nurses' station in the hallway outside Martha's room. The report was "very encouraging," he was told. The patient had been opening her eyes and making sounds. Light therapy would begin soon. Talking? No, no talking yet. Understanding? No signs of that either.

The law clerk and his young assistant continued on the 309 expressway another five miles to the outskirts of Sellersville, where the Rock Hill Mennonite Community was perched upon a hill. Lucy wore a knee-length light blue smock with white flats. *Man, she looks fantastic! Be ready to have your socks blown off, old man.*

Rock Hill was neat and clean but plain. No swimming pools, no tennis or shuffleboard courts were in sight. It had the appearance of an up-scale one-story motel with each room having a fenced-in patio on the ground floor that overlooked the plush gardens. Lucy stared with amazement at the Mennonite ladies, in their long dresses, aprons and bonnets, weeding and watering.

The office secretary pointed them toward a corner apartment where a white-haired man sat with his back to them. "That is Mr. Shultz over there," she offered.

Will waved and shouted in the direction of Bob's patio,

"Hello, it's Will Hoyle, Mr. Shultz." The old man waved also but in the opposite direction.

"Do you know that Mr. Shultz is blind?" The secretary asked.

CHAPTER 16

"Sit down and let me tell you some lies. That's what your grandfather always used to say. He was a real kicker. One of a kind was he and a true blue friend. You understand what I mean young Hoyle? You'd be lucky to have a friend like him." Will sat on a chair opposite his sightless client whose eyes were open, displaying an eerie, hazy blue emptiness as he spoke without a hint of self-consciousness.

Will introduced Lucy to Bob as his assistant and Bob asked her to sit on the arm of his chair so he could touch her face and get to know her. Lucy displayed nothing to suggest that she was fearful of him or disgusted by his looks as she perched herself next to him.

"Yes, Mr. Shultz, I know that the two of you were good friends; that's the reason I'm here. I'm following up with his old friends and clients to make sure that their legal affairs are in order."

"Wow, Lucy, you are a beauty. Great features and perfect skin," Bob said. "How old is she and where is she from?"

"Lucy is nineteen and Dominican. She is helping me with my clients, and I'm helping her with the many challenges she faces." Will explained how Lucy entered the United States and that she was living with an unsettled immigration status. He described the struggles she had faced in Cuba and the Dominican Republic at a young age and how she had overcome them.

"She needs to go to school, get an English tutor, find a place to live, and get a full-time job. She has no money and no identification, and no family or friends here either, apart from me and my family."

Bob appeared moved by Lucy's predicament.

"Talk to me, Lucy. Tell me what you like. I never had a daughter, just two worthless sons. Neither wanted any part of the jewelry business. They were above that. The dumbest thing I did was to send them to college. It ruins a young man. They became too sophisticated to work in a jewelry shop, and now look at them. One makes porn movies in Vegas, and the other runs a collection agency that preys on old people."

Will asked, "Do you ever see them?"

"I used to, but they don't get along. They're both jealous, greedy bums. Each time one comes to visit, the other thinks that his brother is talking me into signing away my money to the other. I can't read so I refuse to sign anything. They're mad at me. To hell with them both."

Bob invited Lucy to watch television inside as he and Will spoke about business. Lucy complied, eagerly asking Will to find a channel with cartoons. After doing so, Will again addressed Bob Shultz.

"Yes, regrettably, many times one's own family is the one with the most to gain and therefore the most conniving. You need to have a fiduciary relationship with a professional whom you can trust to protect your assets. Do you mind telling me about your assets at this time?"

"Hell no, I'm proud of my forty years of honest work at the watch repair table. You know, in the early years, before battery powered watches came about, the money was in the repairing of main springs and stems. It was tedious work with the magnifying glass but good money. It's what eventually took my sight. I have some good investments, but my real wealth is right here in this apartment, and nobody knows it."

All three sat in Bob's living room as the late afternoon became cooler. Lucy sat Indian style on the carpet, laughing at the television while Will and Bob lounged on the couch.

"I have to trust someone, and I'm glad you've come to see me. Can you keep my money and valuables safe from my kids?"

"Yes, of course Bob. We have safe deposit boxes for client's valuables and a bank relationship for safe investments. Moreover, I can prepare the trinity of documents for you that everyone should have."

"Trinity?"

"Yes, a living will, a power of attorney, and a last will and testament."

"My biggest problem is that I don't have beneficiaries. I don't want my rotten sons to inherit a dime, and there aren't any other close relatives alive. That's what happens when you live too damned long. I really can't think of many honest charities either, except maybe for the Lion's Club. Your grandfather and I used to be members together long ago. I think that's where we met. No wait, I'm wrong, it was when he came to me for an estate jewelry appraisal for one of his clients. But anyway, that's pretty ironic, huh? I helped to raise money to assist the blind only to go blind myself. I often think about that." *Yeah. No good deed goes unpunished.*

"You are absolutely right about those so-called charities, Bob. How many times have you heard about the starving kids on TV with flies buzzing around their heads and eating mush with their fingers? Very touching and made so you'll feel guilty for being an American, right? Who gets the money? The promoters. The kids, if they really exist, get zilch. There are millions of young people right here in this country, like Lucy for example, who could use the help, and it would actually make a difference." Will glanced at Lucy who was engrossed watching a "Gilligan's Island" rerun and eating Hershey Kisses from a bowl on Bob's coffee table.

"Will, do me a favor, and go down the hallway to our left and into the first room on your left. It's my bedroom. Under the bed is a wooden chest. Please bring it here so you can take a look inside while you're here. I haven't opened it for years, and there might be some important things for you to be made aware of inside that box."

Will went to the room, where he found a wooden chest carved from solid mahogany that he had to wrestle from under Bob's bed. As he carried it to the living room Will remarked on the weight of the box, asking,

"What is this, your rock collection?"

"In a manner of speaking, yes," replied Bob. "Now if you don't mind, slide the ottoman over here and put the box on it so you can take a look inside. I haven't been able to open it since my wife died. The number to scroll to is 1960. That was the year that I opened my first jewelry store."

As soon as Will lined up the four numbers across the brass dial, the lid popped open an inch or two.

"Now before you open it all the way, look at this eighteen carat gold ring on my finger and tell me how much you think it's worth." Bob slipped it off and held it out for Will to take. "It weighs four ounces and has three two carat diamonds. How much would you say?"

"Gee, I really don't know, three thousand maybe?"

"Try more like ten, my boy. Gold is thirteen hundred an ounce, and the diamonds are worth about two grand each. Ten grand, retail, is what I'd ask for in my shop. Now open my treasure chest."

The inch-thick wood lifted slowly because of the weighty gems attached to its lid. Will was awed by the gleam of more than a dozen necklaces dangling from fabric straps woven into the emerald green velvet lining of the jewelry chest, all rich in diamonds and other precious gems. Strands of pearls clung to the corners and edges of the lid, and gold broaches with gems were pinned to every available piece of unclaimed velvet. The bottom four inches of the box held smaller pieces, most of which were wrapped in tissue paper or stowed in tiny cloth bags with drawstrings. Bracelets, watches, earrings and finger rings had been nestled together, creating the look of a treasure trove to Will. He tapped Lucy's shoulder and motioned for her to move next to Bob where she could see into the chest.

The teen had been told about gems and jewels, and her teacher once showed the class a picture of a Persian fairy whose dress was made of gold, but she had never seen such treasures in reality. Lucy stared at the jewels in amazement as the jeweler fondled each necklace until he was able to identify a solid gold choker supporting eight one carat diamonds spaced an inch apart. Bob held it out and placed it around Lucy's neck saying, "It's yours, sweetheart."

CHAPTER 17

He had spied on them and had them under surveillance the whole day. The ex-security guard turned private eye had arrived at the office of Hoyle, Hoover, and Hoyle just in time to see the car backing out of the parking lot. He had followed the MGB on the hunch that the young driver was the son of Tilly's boyfriend. From the lot to Oak Park to get Lucy, to Grandview Hospital, to the Rock Hill Mennonite Community, and back to Martha's the rented black Chrysler had tailed the red roadster before it was finally given a rest across the street from Martha Kellner's house. Frankie Geyser had been exhausted after a marathon drive on I-95 from Florida to Pennsylvania, only to find it necessary to tail Hoyle all around Bucks County. He was ready for a hot burger and a cold beer.

    The GPS on his dash provided directions to the nearest bar, Mickey's Tavern, located in the Borough of Hatfield. Geyser watched the MGB back out of Martha's driveway, leaving Lucy in the house, he presumed, for the night. His obsession with Lucy had become a lustful desire he could not suppress. *Is she alone in there? Is the boyfriend coming back? Better give it some time. There's no rush now that I know where you are, my sexy little chica.*

Within moments after stepping out of the rental in front of Mickey's, Frankie began to sweat. It had been the hottest day of the year, and the darkness settling in didn't seem to be having the usual cooling effect. White smoke that poured out of the rusty exhaust fan protruding from the bar's wall drifted the scent of fried food past the ex-cop's nostrils as he stiffly waddled inside. After ordering a Bud, a "Kick Mick" burger special, and a side of cheese fries, Frankie pulled a Slim Jim from a clip rack and headed toward the mens' room. Inside and seated, he took a bite off the spicy stick of dried beef and made a call on his cell phone. The national anthem tingled on Jeffery's phone five times, as it sat on his bunk in the guardhouse before the call went to voice mail.

An annoyed Sarge left a message. "Hey, Whippel, where the hell are you? You gotta pick up when I call. I got news for you about your girl. I found her! I know where she lives, and I followed her all day. She went joy riding with the Hoyle kid in his flashy sports car, top down and all. You should have seen them lovin' it up; cute couple, I gotta say. But your girl's new guy is using her to do his clients. I saw her with my own eyes, sitting on some old dude's lap as he fondled her face and body. I even took a photo with my phone, and I'm going to send it to you. It's a real touching scene. Hey, that was pretty good. A touching scene, get it? But what choice does she have, being illegal and all? Call me now."

He ate a quick bite and drank a bottle of beer from the

six-pack he had bought before he left Mickey's as he returned to Martha's neighborhood. Even though cold air was blasting from the dashboard vents, perspiration was trickling down Frankie's chest and back as he parked two blocks from the house, on the opposite side of the front street, in front of a vacant lot with bushes lining the sidewalk. After he had consumed half of the burger and fries, Frankie rolled his paunch off the driver's seat and pulled himself up by the doorframe. With Slim Jims in one hand and the cardboard carrier of beer in the other, he made his way in the dark to the rear of Martha Kellner's home.

A weeping willow tree in the back yard provided the perfect cover for spying on Lucy. He was excited to see the windows open and the curtains drawn to welcome what little breeze there was. He had an unobstructed view of the kitchen and of the dining room where Lucy stood, leaning over a dining table. She had exchanged her summer dress for a skin-tight tee and a pair of short-shorts that exposed her long, tan legs. Frankie blinked his puffy eyes, to make sure he wasn't hallucinating, as he sucked on a bottle of Miller and bit off a chunk of beef jerky. He could feel himself getting hard and dizzy from his intense desire equal only to that he had experienced before with the Mexican girls.

As the private eye crawled to the window on his hands and knees to get a closer look, he could hear music and Lucy's voice singing in Spanish with a Caribbean steel band. When Frankie reached the back wall he placed a hand against it, unzipped his shorts, and began rising to his feet, hoping to look through the kitchen window, but the sudden ringing of his cell phone made him return to the ground as he placed the device on "vibrate." *It must be that Whippel jerk. Now he decides to call me back!* Geyser's phone continued to pulsate in his pocket as he crawled back toward the willow tree and tried to close his pants, but the zipper pinched his most sensitive skin, which made him roll onto his back in agony. *Oh, Whippel, you dumbass! How could he keep calling me at a time like this?* Again and again the cell shook with calls from Jeffery which Frankie intentionally ignored as he grinned with pleasure at the thought of Whippel's worry, panic, and frustration. *Sweat it out, you dummy; maybe you'll learn to answer when the boss man calls.*

The ex-cop crawled a second time to the wall of Martha's house for a look at Lucy. With visions of her gyrating to the steely Latin music, he crouched beneath the window and inched his fingers up to the window, until he was almost high enough to peek inside. His heart raced, beating hard for a glimpse of the nineteen year old as his eyes peered over the sill. Just as they did so, Frankie saw two large eyes staring back at him on the other side of the window screen. A loud screech struck his ears and he saw an orange cat leap over the sink and onto the tile floor. The feline raced through the dining room between Lucy's dancing feet, causing her to stumble, and Frankie ran as fast as his chubby legs could carry him. Around the Keller house he stomped to the street in front, stopping only when he had reached the rental car. Panting and coughing, he fumbled in his pants pockets for the car keys. *They're not here! Where the hell are they?* His hands slapped at his sweat-soaked shirt and shorts. He dropped to the ground and began patting the street in the dark in a futile attempt to find them. *The tree. They probably fell out under the tree when I was trying to answer Whippel's call.*

Lucy had collected Mitsy into her arms and walked to the back door to investigate the cause of the feline's fright. She squinted into the dark yard, relying on the inside kitchen lights for illumination. Everything seemed normal, with the exception of a big dog eating something under a tree.

"Oh, I see what scare you Mitsy but no to worry. *El perro grande* no can get you here in *casa.*" Mitsy became calm and Lucy had returned to the dining room and her music by the time Frankie tiptoed back around the house.

He had approached cautiously until he heard the guitars clanging and Lucy singing, then he crossed the yard to search for his abandoned possessions. Just as he felt the weeping branches touch his head he heard a growl. The P.I. froze in his steps and stared into the center of the tree where he spotted a large beast flashing its fangs at him and giving a throaty, menacing warning. The animal was eating the leftover Slim Jims that Frankie had discarded under the willow near the remaining beer bottles; about a foot away laid the keys to the Chrysler. Geyser remained still until the jittery dog returned its attention to the food, then he inched toward the keys. The animal snarled and snapped its teeth. Frankie pointed his cell phone at the dog and touched "camera" on the pad, causing the device to flash in the dog's eyes. The dog flinched and backed away some, so Frankie continued flashing photos until he was able to move to his items and retrieve them all, except for the Slim

Jims. Frankie flashed and flashed ever closer to the dog's face until it cowered away with its tail tucked between its hind legs. Frankie laughed. *Ha! Threaten me, will you? You're messing with the wrong dude, you smelly piece of crap.* His cell began buzzing again as Frankie collected the beer carrier and keys and began walking toward the car. He pressed Ignore. *Suffer, Whippel, you pansy.*

Safe in the rental, Frankie gulped down a warm beer and was finishing his burger and cold, leftover fries when he saw someone walking toward him in the dark. He leaned closer to the windshield and squinted his eyes in an effort to better see the approaching figure. It appeared to be a woman carrying a baby. As the image became clearer, Frankie began mumbling to himself. "It can't be her, it can't be her. She's in Arizona, she can't be here!"

As the woman reached his rental car, she stepped from the sidewalk onto the street and halted within inches of its front bumper, Frankie recognized her torn clothing and bruised face. The baby in her arms was crying uncontrollably and Frankie began yelling at the mother, "stop it from crying, stop it or I'll kill you both!"

"Please don't hurt my baby. I do what you wanting."

Frankie saw his hands ripping off the woman's blouse as she sobbed in silence, covering her mouth with her hands, and he watched as the woman bled from his blows to her head. "Stop, stop, stop!" Frankie screamed with his head buried in his hands.

After the visions disappeared, Frankie discovered that his

body was drenched from perspiration. He started the car, cranked-up the air conditioning and slowly drove to his motel for a shower and, he hoped, much needed sleep without nightmares.

CHAPTER 18

"Jeffery has disappeared! We've searched everywhere on the island and Fort Jefferson. He's gone, and so is the skiff."

Winston Hoyle III had never heard his girlfriend, Tilly, sound so desperate. "What skiff?"

"The Cubans' boat. It was tied up on the beach waiting for the Coast Guard to come for it." They had spoken every morning before Tilly's first tour and before Winner's first meeting, but she had never called him before.

"Don't panic, sweetheart. I'll call my counterpart, Victor Posada, the Florida A.G., then the Park Service, the Coast Guard, and the Civil Air Patrol to be on the lookout for Jeffery. Don't worry, he'll be found. Did you try his cell phone?"

"Yes, but it might be dead because I found his USB cable on his bunk in the guardhouse. I also found a note and I have it with me. I'll read it":

"Dear Tilly, I hope you don't hate me for it, but I have to leave without saying goodbye. It is an emergency. I can't tell you where or why I'm going but I'll call you when I can. Thank you for being a great friend to Lucy and me. Jeffery."

A tear had rolled down Matilda Jewsel's face as she read the note. "I'm afraid that he went looking for Lucy. He told me how much he missed her and that he had fallen in love with her at first sight. He said that surviving the ordeal with Frankie Geyser convinced him that they had been destined to be together. I don't know what the emergency could be unless he has spoken to Lucy somehow, and she told him she was in trouble. Have you spoken to Will about how she's doing up there with him?"

"Yes, but not today. I'll call him first thing and follow up with law enforcement efforts to locate Jeffery."

"Thank you, Winner; you are my lover, my best friend, and my go-to man. What more could a girl ask for?"

"Thank you, my love, I'll call you later with an update" *and to break the news about running for governor. You've had enough shocking news for one morning.*

Will and Wayne were comparing notes from their "Wills and Estates 101" lectures about powers of attorney, living wills, and administrative duties of an executor when his father called. Will answered, using the speakerphone on the desk for Wayne to listen also.

"Good morning, Will. Something important has come up that concerns Lucy. Is she okay?"

"Yes, Dad, as a matter of fact she is having the time of her life living in the Kellner house with Martha's cat. I have bought her new clothing, and she has gone with me to visit some clients. One old guy even gave Lucy a gold necklace. *Not to mention the chest of jewels that's under my desk.* We've even had dinner together, Lucy and I."

"So, she's not upset about anything? Nothing has happened to frighten her? You didn't try to hit on her?"

"Of course I tried, but she told me she already has a boyfriend, and she's fine."

"Yes, I know; that's why I'm asking. Apparently her boyfriend, one Jeffery Whippel, left his post at Fort Jefferson National Park to find Lucy. Tilly's not certain about that, but she can't think of any other reason for him to have deserted his position as a park ranger. So please be on the lookout for the guy; I wouldn't say anything to Lucy until we're sure about what he's up to."

"Will do, Dad, and we'll be checking on Lucy later today again, so don't be concerned. If we detect any problem at all, you'll be the first to know." Father and son thanked each other as they concluded the conversation.

"Wow, Will," Wayne remarked as Will pressed the speaker key, "I had no freaking idea how exciting it could be practicing Wills and Estates Law. What's going to happen next?"

"Well, Wayne, there is another matter that I haven't discussed with anyone, not even my dad, so I hope you can keep this to yourself *until I need you to vouch for me at my trial.* When dad ran for reelection as A.G., old Chet was still his campaign treasurer and senile as hell. Hoover was handing out money from the campaign account to anyone who'd ask. He even signed blank checks for people. Only God *and I* know to whom they were made payable. Yesterday dad asked me to take over as treasurer for his gubernatorial campaign, so this morning I got here early to look over the books and discovered Chet's handy-work."

"Governor! Holy shit, Will, when did this happen? I haven't read anything about it."

"He hasn't announced publically, and I just found out yesterday. I don't want to tell him that the campaign account is short about four hundred grand because he's going to need millions to run and the preliminary bills are already mounting. Those are advance payment items, such as billboards, TV spots, radio ads, and P.R."

"You're going to have to tell him sometime, and how do you plan to make up the difference?"

"I was thinking, Wayne, what if some of the firm's most wealthy long-time clients were to donate to the 'Hoyle for Governor Committee'?"

CHAPTER 19

He had waited until after midnight to slide the weary skiff into the tropical waters surrounding the island. The boat's motor had proven simple for him to repair, and with the right fuel mixture and clean motor oil the park ranger was able to get it running again. His decision to leave the Tortugas and Fort Jefferson in search of Lucy was made when his frantic calls, in response to Frankie's message, went unanswered throughout the day and into the night. He had confided in no one, not even Tilly, and all six remaining employees of the National Park Service had retired for the evening long before he had pushed off.

His plan consisted of little more than heading north to Pennsylvania by any means possible. An army-style duffel bag lay on the floor of the skiff, stuffed with clothing, food, some light bedding, and two small American flags. Jeffery had taken his wallet and a few hundred dollars with him, but his uniform, badge and pistol were left on his bunk along with his hand written note to his friend, Tilly Jewsel.

After he navigated the heavy boat through a maze of coral reefs during the darkest hours, Jeffery reached deeper water when the sun began to show itself. As the craft puttered on, blazing rays of light burst over the horizon, transforming thousands of tiny ripples of water into what seemed to be a sea of turquoise-colored diamonds. The rays of the sun struck his face and temporarily blinded his eyes, causing the young ranger to feel a sense of tranquility he had never experienced. *Heaven cannot be greater than this. I can't wait to bring Lucy here to see this.*

Jeffery had not been aware of the seawater sloshing around his boots. Scraping over jagged coral throughout the night had taken its toll on the wooden craft, damaging its underbelly just enough to create seepage. He had nothing with which to bail the salty pool beneath him, and he became concerned that his transportation might not make it all the way to Key West. At full throttle, the skiff wasn't moving much faster than Jeffery could walk, but what he could see below the surface of the shallow sea was spectacular. Wrecks of sailing ships of yore lay seductively on the ocean's floor, and schools of rainbow-colored fish zigged and zagged above them. Stingrays performed a water ballet as they investigated his craft, and occasionally a shark would lumber by looking for an easy meal. Jeffery's boat began to list to one side as its motor strained, laboring its way toward Key West, still many miles away.

After another hour of motoring, with the sea lapping inside his craft, Jeffery spotted a large, slowly approaching cabin cruiser, fitted with outriggers and fishing gear. Two men stood at the stern studying the yacht's wake as it began to circle about seventy-five yards ahead, Jeffery estimated. Ranger Whippel twisted the handle of the tiller until the skiff's propeller ceased turning. The wind and tide were favorable, pushing the drifting boat toward the yacht, as Jeffery removed one of the American flags from his duffel and began waving it at the two men. He then began to shout, "Ahoy there mates! I'm an American, a friend. I need help." The men looked his way, and as the skiff drifted closer he could read the words "Bertram 65" inscribed on the yacht's hull. Jeffery waved the flag again and yelled, "I'm sinking and I need help!"

Seconds before his dirty craft would have bumped into the shiny yacht, a darkly tanned man with white beard and hair extended a boat hook and harmlessly guided the flooded vessel to its side at the yacht's stern. Jeffery got a closer look at the man and saw that his chest was also white with hair and that a blue captain's hat sat tightly upon his head. Jeffery stared at him thinking, *Wow, he's a dead ringer for Ernest Hemingway.*

After tying up, Hemingway lifted a rifle with a spear attached to its barrel from the yacht's deck, pointed it at Jeffery's face, and ordered him to strip naked.

CHAPTER 20

The name of the big yacht was *Moonglow*. Jeffery remembered seeing it inscribed in gold leaf script on the boat's transom while he sat naked in the sinking skiff. Captain Hemingway had made him strip at the point of his spear gun while a toothless, darkly tanned crew member used a boat hook to steer Jeffery's boat to the stern of the yacht. The latter wore a handgun at his side. While shedding his clothing, Jeffery explained his dire circumstances. He spoke rapidly, hoping to dissuade his rescuers from shooting him, telling them that he was a park ranger from the Tortuga Islands and that he was looking for a refugee from Cuba. The two salty dogs spoke in Spanish, not realizing that their intruder could understand what they were saying. Captain Hemingway ordered Toothless not to harm Jeffery for the time being and said, "Having a federal ranger aboard might come in handy if there's trouble."

They dragged Jeffery aboard *Moonglow*, forced him to go below into a large cabin area, and placed him in a head. The tiny lavatory was clean, with a strong odor of disinfectant emanating from the plastic toilet bowl. He had to crouch to prevent his head from bumping the ceiling, and after hearing a latching sound at the door, he sat upon the commode and tried turning the doorknob. Locked. He called to the men, "Why are you doing this? I am a friend. I'm not here to cause you any trouble. I just need help!" Silence.

It seemed as though only a few moments of quiet drifting had passed when suddenly *Moonglow*'s powerful engines roared into action. Jeffery could feel the thrust of the propellers and the vibration of the cruiser's hull as the heavy yacht plowed through the tropical waters to a destination unknown to him. The young park ranger felt fear beginning to control his thoughts. *What if they are criminals? Maybe this yacht is stolen. I don't want to die here, sitting naked.*

After a few moments had passed, Jeffery relaxed slightly and began thinking about his ranger training. *If you can keep your head when all those around you are losing theirs, you are a man my boy. Yes, I need to keep my head. Think! How do I get out of this predicament? First, I need to get out of this cramped washroom, but I need some tools.* He continued to sit on the toilet seat while he searched two tiny drawers where he found a tube of Crest toothpaste, two toothbrushes, a box of Band-Aids, washcloths, towels, and a new bar of Safeguard soap. Under a stainless sink bowl was a small closet that contained a handful of cans. There he found what he needed standing upright in a plastic holder at the back of the vanity: a long-handled toilet brush, the tool he could use to free himself from the makeshift brig. Jeffery's mechanical abilities took over and he methodically untwisted the wire brush, removed all the bristles, then straightened the wire and inserted its end into a keyhole on the inside of the washroom door. From the sound he had heard earlier when Toothless locked him inside, Jeffery had concluded that the latch was a simple sliding mechanism that could be easily pried open. Once he had inserted the tip of the wire as far as it would go, Jeffery pressed it hard to bend the tip slightly. The other end of the wire was still attached to the wooden handle, which he used to turn the wire clockwise. The process was slow, but after about fifteen minutes Jeffery managed to dislodge the sliding latch just enough to clear its harness. He carefully turned the doorknob and slowly opened the washroom door.

Jeffery listened for the sound of movement or voices coming from the spacious cabin, but the only sounds were those of the engines and the sea. When he emerged from the head no one was in sight. He exhaled with a huge sigh of relief, not realizing that he had been holding his breath. Then he saw the unexpected. The original living area of the plush yacht was piled high with crates and cardboard boxes. The living area of *Moonglow*, which looked like it had once been a beautifully furnished room, had been transformed into an expensive floating storage room. The stark walls of boxes covered more than half the sitting area where once had stood comfortable chairs, a television, tables, lamps, and draperies. The open space separating the crates from the galley, head, and gangway to the deck above contained three rolled-up sleeping bags, knapsacks stuffed with clothing, cartons of

Marlboro cigarettes, and an assortment of partially empty liquor bottles. A long yellow rain slicker hung from a hook on the wall next to Jeffery's washroom prison. He slipped his long, muscular arms into its sleeves and snapped the many metal hooks in front to cover his large, naked frame.

The hatchway from the aft deck above, through which he had been led into the cabin, had carpeted steps leading up to a teak wood door. The door was closed and, Jeffery assumed, locked. He was reluctant to attempt opening it, fearing detection by his two abductors. *But there must be at least three people because someone had to have been driving this boat when I first spotted it.* Feeling safe, for the moment, Ranger Whippel decided to investigate the cargo and quickly determined that there were dozens of boxes with no visible markings on them. *It must be contraband; illegal goods of some kind. Why else would they strip me of everything and lock me up? That's why they're armed and threatening! Think! Think!*

Jeffery's cell phone and clothing had been confiscated by Captain Hemingway and, he surmised, probably thrown overboard. He desperately wanted to call for help, so he searched the area for a phone or a ship-to-shore radio, which he had been taught to use by the park service. Neither was to be found, so he decided upon a plan of action. *What am I going to do when they come to check on me? How do I really know what they are up to? I've got to set a trap for them. Look in the boxes; I need to know for sure what they are carrying.*

Jeffery's first move was to re-latch the washroom door so Toothless, if he returned, would assume that his prisoner was still inside the head. Secondly, he decided to open one of the crates located in the row of containers farthest from the entryway. There he could work unseen by anyone arriving, and it was unlikely that his tampering would be noticed until the cargo was removed. He hadn't yet decided what to do if one of his captors came for him.

It was a tight squeeze for him to maneuver around and between the rows of boxes, but Jeffery soon discovered that the walls of cargo were sturdy and the boxes heavy. So he sidestepped his large body between the last row and the far wall. As he moved, he noticed a door that obviously led to an additional forward compartment closer to the boat's bow. *If somebody comes, maybe I can scoot in there to hide. Maybe it even leads to another way out!* He practically became wedged in the corner as he turned to look around. Everything was the same as when he had begun his investigation. The cruiser's engines were still moaning strongly as the ocean water exploded past its hull. Jeffery was just tall enough to see over the top of the highest box on the pile in front of him, and he checked to be certain that the hatch door from the stern deck remained tightly closed.

Ranger Whippel used his strong fingers to rip into one of the crates.

CHAPTER 21

Oak Park

He sipped on Sprite through a straw as he ogled Lucy through his binoculars. Somewhere he had heard that Sprite worked well to relieve a hangover, and a hangover he had. He had drunk too much the night before while being exhausted from his long drive north, and his sixty-five dollar motel room sat a mere one hundred yards from the Pennsylvania Turnpike. When he did sleep, his re-occurring nightmares returned to jar him awake in a cold sweat. In the morning, he could barely keep his eyes open and his stomach felt queasy, but his obsession with Lucy had compelled him to return to Martha's Oak Park home in the morning.

It was a warm, spring-like day, and Lucy had emerged from inside to garden on the sunny side of the house. Frankie sat in the rented Chrysler on the far side of Park Avenue in front, peering at her through powerful lenses. It made him feel as though he were standing next to her long, dark hair, pink tank top and cut-off jeans as she squatted, weeding a flowerbed. He wanted her desperately. He had to have her, but he needed a plan. *I could disguise myself so she wouldn't recognize me, or I could wear a ski mask and grab her.* Frankie's eyes widened as Lucy stood to stretch. *Or fake a robbery when she goes inside, tie her up, and put her in my trunk! Yeah, that's the ticket; how's she going to fight against my gun? I need you now, sexy chica.*

Sarge might have experienced a total loss of control over his actions at that moment if it hadn't been for a patrol car appearing at the corner. Frankie started the car's engine, slowly pulled away from the curb, and waved to the cop as he passed. Breathing a sigh of relief, the ex-guard drove out of Martha's neighborhood directly to the office of Hoyle, Hoover, and Hoyle.

Inside the upstairs conference room the two law clerks reviewed files and discussed clients in preparation for their day's work while Evelyn typed away downstairs, keeping an eye on Chester Hoover. Will was elated to finally have a friend with whom he could share his tale of woe and vent his frustrations.

"Here's the summary of all that's happened in the last nine months, Wayne. My boss, Chet, suffered a stroke last fall, one client has died, another is on her death bed, a blind client has fallen for an illegal immigrant under my care, a park ranger has gone AWOL in Florida and is looking for her, my father has announced his candidacy for governor, and I've just been made treasurer of a campaign fund that's four hundred thousand short. Oh, yes, and a Colombo wannabe is sniffing around asking questions just because I didn't answer a client's phone call before she died."

Wayne shook his head saying "and I thought I'd just be sitting around drafting wills, but I can see that I'm about to have more pressing duties. So, now I have questions. What are you doing when you visit clients? What do they need us for? What happens if the client doesn't have any relatives to serve as their surrogate, attorney-in-fact, or executor? The case in point is your client Martha Kellner. Who gets the lucky job of deciding when to pull the plug?"

"All good questions, Wayne. In each case, Chester had originally written the client's living will, power of attorney, and will. All I do is update them to meet their current needs; Hoover stays as the drafter because we're not licensed yet. My name doesn't appear anywhere as having drafted any documents. If a surrogate needs to be named, a power given, or an executor changed, I usually just name the firm. That way, you me, and Evelyn can take care of the client's needs without us being personally involved and acting as Chester's alter ego until he recovers." *There is no chance of that happening.*

"So, as long as Mr. Hoover is alive and able to approve what we are doing we can carry on doing the work behind the scenes as law clerks."

"Right, Wayne. That's why it's so critical for us to find the clients who are living alone without family support."

Wayne was shaking his head again. "Wow, it's a shame that there are so many old ones out there who don't have anyone that cares about them."

"Yeah, it's a sin what's happened to our society. It used to be that family took care of family. Today the kids get their parents to sign everything over to them, leaving them penniless, and then stick them in a home, hoping that Medicaid will pick up the bill. We won't do that, Wayne, and Martha Kellner is a perfect example. I was prepared to make sure she lived in her home for the rest of her life. I was planning to have Lucy care for her, and that's the reason Lucy is living there now."

"Wasn't she taken off life support? Is she still alive?"

"I had them put her back on after she responded to Lucy the other day. That reminds me; would you take Lucy to see her at Grandview Hospital today?" *I sure as hell don't want to be there if the old bag wakes up.*

"Wow, really Will? I'd love to. May I use your MG? I'd be embarrassed to make a honey like her ride in my piece of crap."

"Sure, I'll give you directions; just be real careful with both of those babies."

Wayne found his way through the office to the back door that led to the rear parking lot. As he passed the kitchen doorway he glanced in and saw Chester Hoover slumped over in his wheelchair. His secretary, Evelyn, was making coffee at the counter. He entered and said, "Hello Mr. Hoover, I'm Wayne, Will's friend." The invalid attorney made no movements and didn't respond.

"I'm sorry, Wayne," she said, but Mr. Hoover hasn't spoken since his stroke."

"Oh. Will told me that Mr. Hoover was still able to kind of oversee things in the office."

In an effort to avoid contradicting Will, Evelyn responded, "well, I suppose that Will is expecting Mr. Hoover to recover and, after all, they have worked closely together off and on for three years. Will probably knows better."

Frankie Geyser was calling Jeffery in vain as he sat in surveillance in the alley behind the Hoyle Building when Wayne emerged. He was surprised to see someone different driving the red sports car as he followed it out of the parking lot. *Now who are you, curly, red head, and where are you going? Let's find out.*

CHAPTER 22

The bank's receptionist told Will that Mr. Black was in a meeting but to hold anyway because she had been instructed to interrupt him whenever Mr. Hoyle called. The eventual heir to the firm of Hoyle, Hoover and Hoyle smiled proudly and thought, *money talks baby. Money talks.*

The banker's voice came through the speakerphone moments later.

"Good afternoon, Attorney Hoyle; what can I do for you this fine day?" *Another mistaken identity, I could get used to this.*

"Hello, Barry, I need to make some money transfers."

"Absolutely," Barry replied. "From what account would you like to transfer?"

"Accounts, Barry, accounts: three in all. The Dunbar estate account, for which I received the short certificates today and will mail one to you; the Kellner financial management account, using the power of attorney you have on file; and the Robert Shultz savings account we opened last week, using the power of attorney for him as well."

"No problem, Mr. Hoyle. Can you tell me what accounts will be receiving the transfers?"

"Account, Barry, just one account. If you check your records, you will find an account opened many years ago entitled 'Hoyle Political Action Committee.' Each of the firm's three clients I have named wishes to donate fifty thousand dollars toward ensuring that Pennsylvania continues to have good governance. Now isn't that an outstanding and worthy cause? Tax deductible too."

Will received a call from Bob Shultz's phone at Rock Hill Retirement Community. The elderly blind man usually just pressed the "call" button on the cell phone Will had given him, and, as Will had hoped, all calls went to him. Bob's Mennonite caregiver had found him unconscious on the living room floor of his independent-living apartment unit. He had been transferred to the total-care unit.

Awake and alert again, the retired jeweler related the events of the morning. He had tripped and fallen while walking from his patio into his living room because he couldn't locate his cane after having risen from a folding chair. The staff told the nurses that he had struck his head on the TV stand as he fell. Bob confided in Will that he was feeling weak and a little confused. He wanted to be sure that his estate was in order should something happen to him. It was clear to Will that Bob had forgotten about signing the papers for him the week before.

Will decided that he needed to console his wealthy client and make certain that Bob didn't contact another attorney to review the situation. The retirement home might even have a lawyer they could refer him to.

"Hey Bob, do you remember my pretty island girl assistant, Lucy? I brought her to visit you just last week."

Bob Shultz was silent for a moment before he spoke. Then suddenly he blurted out, "Yeah, yeah, oh yeah! She's a honey of a girl. How is she? Will she visit me again sometime?"

"How about this afternoon? Would you like her to visit you this afternoon?"

"That would be great. Do you think she likes me? Wants to see me again? I'd like to give her some jewelry; some really good jewelry. I have it hidden in my bedroom." Will didn't remind Bob that he had already given Lucy a necklace and him the jewelry chest.

"That's very generous of you, Bob, I'm sure that Lucy would be very appreciative. She's poor, as you know. I've even been trying to raise money for her to attend college, but it's been difficult."

"I can help her. Just have her come visit me, please, and thank you, thank you."

"I will try to contact her, Bob. She is with my partner right now, but maybe he can take her there to see you now or soon. Okay?"

"Yes, that's great. Thanks, Winston." *Here we go again.*

Wayne's iPhone played a Taylor Swift tune when Will called them. Wayne loved Taylor Swift. They were in the produce section, squeezing avocados to determine which ones were ripe. Wayne agreed to drive Lucy to Rock Hill, having been given directions by Will, and when he told Lucy where they were about to go she seemed genuinely happy.

"Señor Bob is nice man and mi liking he *mucho*," she said.

"He is a nice man and I like him a lot," Wayne corrected. They packed the tiny trunk of Will's roadster and headed for route 309. A black Chrysler followed them onto the expressway. Frankie couldn't understand why Wayne wasn't returning to the Kellner house with the groceries. Where were they going? Had the driver decided to shake him? *No chance of that happening.*

Frankie couldn't believe it when the MG turned into the driveway of the Rock Hill Mennonite Community. He surmised that the old guy was paying weekly for a little love, and he became jealous. The private eye parked his rental in a used car lot across the street and waited, desperately wanting to know what Lucy was doing with the geezer. *I gotta get her out of here. She's mine.*

CHAPTER 23

Cuban rum, cigars, and marijuana seedlings, all illegal imports to the U.S.; this boat's name should be Moonshine, *not* Moonglow, *and these guys are bootlegging crooks.* Jeffery had opened five boxes while the yacht continued its race through the waters of the Atlantic and afterward decided to explore the forward cabin.

The door to the room had been locked on the outside, which made his entry simpler than his escape from the toilet. The chamber was dark with the exception of a sliver of sunlight streaking across the carpeted floor. A bulging canvas bag with a drawstring opening lay on the deck of the room, and he noticed a green snout protruding from the small opening. Jeffery was able to identify the creature's lumpy nose from his ranger school zoology course. Crocodiles! Not just one, but at least a few. How many exactly he couldn't immediately determine, but he could tell from the size of the one trying to wiggle out of the bag that there were at least two more inside, packed tightly together.

Upon closer examination Jeffery saw that the reptile's jaw was held closed with a wide, thick rubber band, and as an appendage appeared, he saw that the animal's claws had been duct tapped together so that it couldn't rip its way out of the sack. He could scarcely believe that what he was looking at was real. The scaly beast's bulging eyes were frightening, and Jeffery began to imagine what would happen if that rubber band around its jaws would break. The crocodile struggled to be free of the bag's pull-cord now tight around its stomach. At that moment, panic had begun screaming through his brain so fiercely that Jeffery hadn't noticed the other five sacks lying on the carpeting deeper inside the cabin's hull. Nor had he seen the body on the "V" berth above them.

It was a Cuban croc, native only to Cuba and endangered. The Cuban crocodile did not grow as large as those found in South America, such as along the Amazon River in Brazil and Peru where an adult male could be twelve feet in length and weigh as much as three hundred pounds. The Cuban crocodile normally grew to about eight feet, including its tail, but some strains were smaller. For this reason, Jeffery couldn't determine whether the creature he was engaging was a baby or one of the smaller varieties.

It was three to four feet long, he estimated, but it seemed to the ranger that a third of that length was jawbone and teeth capable of ripping off a human's hand. His heart raced as he watched the rubber band stretch slightly, exposing teeth, and then snap back into position. He was terrified when he thought that the band could break. His legs shook at the thought of trying somehow to force the beast back into the sack. *Probably the only thing holding it in is the weight of the others inside the sack.*

Jeffery saw something move out of the corner of his left eye. He glanced that way only for a second or two, not wanting to take his sight from the determined crocodile squirming a few feet in front of him. He did this four more times before he could see what was there. More sacks! A chill traveled up his spine. More crocs! A nerve in his neck felt pinched. Then he thought he saw a small body on the cushion that was the bed in the hull cabin. He took a longer look, then there was a loud snap and the black rubber band whizzed by his ear.

The crocodile's jaws and teeth made a sound like the clapping of two enormous hands as they separated and then slammed together, in rapid fire fashion, with the beast biting and hissing at the air as if it wanted to punish anything that came near. Jeffery realized in a moment that the situation was potentially deadly should the croc free itself from its confinement.

Jeffery stood and began ripping off his yellow rubber rain slicker as fast as his hands would move. The croc continued to bite the air and began whipping its head from side to side as it appeared to be inching out of the sack. Just as Jeffery freed his arms from the sleeves of the coat, the crocodile lunged forward and began crawling out of the bag. Only its hind legs remained inside, and Jeffery could see the nostrils of another croc emerging also. The park ranger's adrenalin peaked as he held the raincoat in front of himself, spread wide open, and pounced upon the wriggling crocodile. He was grateful that the duct tape had held together on those treacherous claws as he forced the coat's rubber hood over the fighting animal's nose. Jeffery wrapped his muscular arms around the squirming beast, lifting it off the boat's carpet just high enough to force the long coat all the way around its belly. Jeffery then lay naked, upon the animal's back and remained as motionless as he possibly could. He felt the breath of another bagged croc puffing from its nostrils onto his bare feet. *Dear God, if you're up there and like me even a little bit, please don't let its rubber band break.*

At some place in his course book, though he couldn't remember where, Jeffery recalled reading that an alligator could be put to sleep by rubbing its stomach. He prayed that the same would work on a crocodile as he stroked the angry animal's belly. The park ranger didn't really know how it happened, but within minutes of covering the croc's eyes with the hood of the rain slicker and softly rubbing its stomach, he was able to calm the beast and stuff it back into the thick canvas sack, raincoat and all. He secured the rope to make certain that no others could escape and then lay prone on the deck's carpet, exhaling with relief. Then he suddenly remembered the other bags. He was afraid to move more deeply into the V-berth shaped cabin. The very thought that more crocodiles awaited him made his skin crawl. Jeffery wanted to retreat to the solitude and safety of his toilet cell in the other compartment, but there were problems. For one, he was pretty sure there was a body. For another, he was naked again. *Golly, what to do? What to do? I can't leave somebody in here with these crocs. I can't.*

The portal windows in the side of the hull had been draped

in black cloth and taped. Jeffery could see just well enough to avoid stepping on the other bags as he made his way to one of the windows, but he had to stretch his legs and torso as far as possible to reach it. Balancing himself with one hand on the back of a bench seat, ranger Whippel used his other hand to peel the tape from one portal. Once the drape was pulled to one side, the bright afternoon sun burst into the cabin like a floodlight in the middle of the night.

The yacht's powerful engines seemed to intensify as Jeffery gazed upon the small, huddled body of a girl strapped and tied to a bed. Below her, on the floor, was a bag, smaller than the croc sacks and made from burlap, not canvas. It appeared to contain something large and lumpy; Jeffery wondered what other surprise awaited him. He had no desire to find out, but he knew that he would have to reach the girl. Before that, however, he would have to cover his bare body. The young ranger began searching. There were built-in drawers and closets meant to serve the master bedroom aboard the spacious yacht. As he opened them, many useful things appeared. He found a metal ring holding about one dozen keys, a flashlight and flares, a box of saltines, two bags of Hershey's Kisses, and a closet filled with a variety of clothing, sandals, caps and diving equipment. Jeffery frantically dug through the items until he found a pair of men's shorts with sailboats and an orange golf shirt that would fit.

As he dressed, his eyes darted from the croc sacks to the girl on the bed and then to the door through which he had entered. Thankfully, the boat had continued its breakneck pace and the crew had not yet returned to check on him.

Before making his way across the room to the girl on the bed, Jeffery opened one of the portals by releasing two chrome latches and lifting a hinged glass window to position it like the sun visor on a car's windshield. This invited fresh sea air and a soft salty spray to enter the stuffy cabin. Jeffery inhaled, his chest bulging with every delightful breath. Then he turned toward the slight human form lying motionless in a fetal position.

CHAPTER 24

Ranger Whippel relied upon his training once again by slowing his thoughts and by analyzing the situation. He had to make the best use of the things he had at his disposal. He had to be careful not to step on the crocodile bags, especially since he hadn't found anything to wear on his feet. Most importantly, he wanted a plan of action that wouldn't endanger the girl.

Jeffery stuffed one pocket of his Bermuda shorts with candy Kisses and into the other he put the ring of keys and one flare. Then Jeffery carefully made his way to the other side of the cabin where the small figure lay huddled against a cushion. He stepped over the burlap bag on the floor beneath the berth and climbed upon the bed. A tiny brown-skinned girl, with her thin arms wrapped tightly around her knees, sat shaking, her wrists cuffed like a criminal's and her mouth covered with duct tape. One rope and one leather strap secured her, somehow, to the yacht's hull. When Jeffery touched the girl's head, her shoulders jerked forward in fear.

"I won't hurt you," Jeffery said in Spanish, speaking softly close to her ear. "I am here to save you. Please trust me."

The child kept her head tucked between her knees, and Jeffery's instincts told him that the girl was weeping. He slid closer to her and slowly put his muscular arm around the tiny child's shoulders. She wore only a pale blue tee shirt and a pair of white runner's shorts. Her feet were bare also, so Jeffery held one of his feet above her and said, "Look, I don't have any shoes either. If I was a bad guy would I be walking around in these stupid tourist clothes in bare feet?" He felt the tension in her muscles relax slightly, so he reached into his pocket and grasped a handful of Hershey's Kisses.

Unwrapping one, Jeffery reached under the girl's arms and offered it to her. When she lifted her head, he said, "This is going to hurt" and quickly ripped the duct tape from her lips. The little girl didn't cry out. Instead, she grasped her mouth with both hands and began sobbing.

Jeffery held the slight child in his arms and asked, "*Como se llama, mi niña?*" The girl looked at him for the first time, and Jeffery saw the same beautiful green eyes he had fallen in love with at Fort Jefferson. She responded weakly, "My name is Migelina," Jeffery unwrapped a handful of Kisses and fed them to her one by one as he continued to talk.

"They captured me, stripped me, and locked me in the bathroom in the other cabin," he said as he pointed to the door. "Do you know that in there they have boxes of rum, cigars, and pot?" Migelina said that she had overheard the crew talking as they loaded the contraband. "They plan to sell those things and me to some men in New York and in some place called Philadelphia. They stole me from my town; the big one told the others that he needed a virgin girl. They stole important rocks, too, from the ancient underwater City of the Gods."

Jeffery had heard about an ancient city discovered in 2000 under the waters off the west coast of Cuba. It was thought to be thousands of years old and with granite structures similar in shape to the historic pyramids of the Middle East. Destroyed by a tornado, it became famous in Cuban literature.

Drawing the girl closer, Jeffery hugged her tightly and said nothing for few moments. He waited for her to speak again without being prompted. She did not talk but her eyes flashed around the room in fear as if she was looking for something. Jeffery had to ask, "What are you afraid of? That they will come and find us together?" The girl shook her head *no*. "That the crocodiles will get you?" Migelina responded with a similar shake of her head.

"Then is it me you fear?"

"No, it is the *colebra*."

"Snake? What snake?" Jeffery asked. Then he remembered the burlap bag on the deck beneath them. "Is there a snake in the bag on the floor?"

"Si, Señor. *Una boa grande*."

Ranger Whippel knew a thing or two about snakes. He had three pet snakes as a boy, and on-site training as a ranger cadet had taken him and his classmates to the Florida Everglades for nature study. He had handled American boa constrictors and knew that they were not dangerous to adult humans. He could easily understand, however, how a child could be deathly afraid of such a creature.

"Is that the reason they put the bag near you? Did they threaten you with the snake?" Jeffery calmly asked the girl.

"They told me that if I moved, the snake would hear me and come out of the bag to strangle me."

"Don't worry; I won't let that happen," Jeffery replied, as he stepped onto the floor, bent down, and lifted the bagged boa as if it were a sack of potatoes. The animal squirmed inside until its head was at the tied end of the burlap bag. Jeffery saw its tongue flicker through the tiny gap at the drawstring. Migelina watched in horror and disbelief. "The tongue can't hurt you, Miggy," which he knew in Spanish is an endearing nickname for Migelina, "It only uses it to smell, and I must smell very bad at this point." Miggy showed a nervous smile as the big man gently laid the bag on the deck as far from Miggy and the croc sacks as possible.

When he returned to the girl's side they began trying to unlock her cuffs with the keys he had found. They became frustrated as attempt after attempt failed, but the boat's engines continued to growl loudly so Gomer took his time. Migelina watched him carefully and seemed to be studying him in admiration. Then she said, "look up there" as she pointed, with the palms of her hands together, to some small teak cabinets above them. Only two more keys remained on the ring, and they were much too large for the tiny holes in the handcuffs, so Jeffery stood erect and reached for one of the latched doors. It was locked, but he soon found a key on the ring that fit the lock and slid open a latticed door. Inside Ranger Whippel found two small keys on a string, a fishing knife, a loaded .22 pistol, his wallet, and his cell phone. Jeffery was elated and mumbled, "*gracias a Dios.*"

He became energized by his findings and impulsively planted a kiss on Miggy's forehead. Then, fumbling with the little keys, he unlocked her handcuffs. After that he ripped the blade of the fishing knife through the strap and rope. Migelina was finally free, and she threw her arms around his neck, hugging with all of her tiny might. Jeffery hugged back.

But their euphoria was abruptly interrupted when the roar of the yacht's engines reduced to a rumble. They felt the boat come off plane as its hull dipped forward and the rushing of the sea ceased.

"Oh God," Jeffery whispered to Miggy, "I think we're stopping to refuel. Quick, curl back onto the bed. I'm sorry but I must re-tape your mouth and cuff you again. We need to return to the way it was in case they check on us while we're stopped." Miggy didn't protest and seemed to understand how critical their situation was. She scrambled into the fetal position once again and held her hands together for the cuffing. Jeffery did his best to make her appear undisturbed. Then he lifted the boa bag and returned it to its original position, reached up and closed the cabinet door, stripped off his clothes and shoved them and all other items into the closet.

Standing naked, Ranger Whippel looked around one last time, as a double check, then passed through the door to the main cabin area. He hustled past the rows of boxed contraband and returned to his washroom prison cell. There he once again used the toilet brush wire to re-lock the head's door and waited. *What did I forget?* His worried thoughts made him feel light-headed, or maybe he was just hungry. *Please! Don't let them come or open the closet door in there. Please don't let any harm come to Migelina. Wait! Golly! The raincoat - what if they notice that it's missing?*

It became too late for more worry, as he heard the frightening sound of footsteps and the rattling of a padlock. Jeffery couldn't keep from questioning whether he had done the right thing. Had he made the right decision by having them play possum, or should he have stayed with the girl, ready to fight? He knew that his answer would come within minutes, and he was ready to risk his life to save Migelina if it came to that. He decided that if Hemingway and Toothless opened his toilet door again and gave him reason to think that they might go to the other cabin, he would fight them and rescue the girl. He had to do it.

While the two crewmen were entering the cabin, the yacht's owner and real captain was entering the master cabin through another hatchway. It led from the pilot's helm down into the room where Migelina lay huddled and frightened. Jeffery hadn't noticed the other entrance and believed that he would be able to hear anyone entering the other cabin through the same door he had used. If he heard Hemingway and Toothless go there, he would follow them to make sure that no harm came to Miggy. But they engaged him the same as before, bringing him water and, this time, candy. Before they left Jeffery asked why the boat had stopped, and Toothless told him that they needed to refuel. As he spoke, Jeffery saw Hemingway drink from a bottle of rum and said, "I hope the captain isn't drinking too. That could be dangerous."

"That's none of your business, Lone Ranger, but it so happens that we is goin' ashore here for dinner and waitin' til mornin' to motor on. But don't get no ideas about escapin', cause I'll be back soon to guard the boat and we'll all be here later. Got it?" He flashed Jeffery one of his toothless smiles, then locked the head's door and left. The ranger was preparing to follow until he heard them thumping their way up the steps to the deck. He was puzzled that they hadn't checked Miggy before leaving, but supposed that they probably thought it was impossible for her to free herself. Nevertheless, it did seem odd to him, so he unlocked his prison door and hustled to her cabin. When he heard a door slam from within he rushed inside, ready for a fight. No one was there except Migelina. Jeffery hopscotched his way to the closet, dressed and stepped to her side. "Are you okay?" He removed the duct tape from her mouth.

"Yes, but he came here"

"Who was here?"

"El Pescado. Everyone in our town calls him The Fish because of his long, skinny nose and his beady black eyes."

CHAPTER 25

Private eye Geyser watched and waited for more than an hour for Lucy and Wayne to return to Will's MG from their visit with Bob Schulz. Through his rental's window he saw them as they walked across the parking lot to the car. They were laughing and looking at each other. Lucy was smiling and seemed happy. Frankie felt himself losing control as he slapped the steering wheel in anger.

The law clerk and his charge talked all the way "home" to Martha's house in Oak Park. Their visit with Bob had been more fulfilling than either could have imagined. The sickly, blind jeweler became energized talking to Lucy. The young Dominican spoke to him in her charming "Spanglish," and they all laughed like grade school children as they corrected each other's language misinterpretations. At one point, Lucy sat on the edge of Bob's bed and taught him a Latino song. She sang, in tune, her favorite Louis Guerra ballad, "You Have the Keys to My Heart."

Before his visitors left, Bob promised to pay for Lucy's

education for as long as it might take or cost. He requested that Wayne be sure to put that into his will also. The old man beamed with joy as Lucy kissed him on each cheek as they rose to leave. Bob Schultz shouted after her, as she and Wayne walked through the hallway, "I'll buy you a new car too, sweetie, when you're old enough to drive." Wayne interpreted for Lucy, which caused her to return to the jeweler's doorway to tell him that she really would like to have a horse. The late afternoon sun turned yellow as it followed the roadster back to Oak Park.

So now he's going to try and make her. Frankie watched Wayne lift a bottle of wine from the back of the car after he and Lucy had returned and unloaded at Martha's home. *So help me, I'll kill him if I have to. I didn't come all this way to hand her over to a loser like him.*

In the kitchen Wayne poured two glasses of Merlot and showed Lucy how to toast. They clicked glasses, drank, and laughed some more about their fun time spent with Bob Schultz.

"Old Bob really likes you, Lucy, and so do I. In fact, I think you are the most beautiful girl I ever met. Do you understand?"

"*Si, gracias.*" Lucy hadn't understood, word for word, but as Wayne moved closer she read his body language as indicating an intent she couldn't identify but disliked.

"Good." Wayne grabbed Lucy's shoulders firmly and attempted to pull her toward his body. Lucy instinctively jutted both of her forearms upward with great force knocking his grip from her body saying, "Por favor, no toca mi!"

She then turned around, hastily opened a drawer beneath the kitchen counter, and grabbed the first utensil she saw. Wielding a large, silver platter fork, Lucy began warning Wayne in Spanglish to stay away as she recalled her encounter with the man on the Cuban skiff. *Why do men want to attack me? What am I doing to them to cause this?*

"I'm sorry!" Wayne said as he backed away. "I didn't mean to scare you and I'd never hurt you."

Again, Lucy didn't comprehend all that Wayne had said but quickly realized that Wayne hadn't meant to harm her; still, she couldn't understand why he had touched her. "*Yo tengo un novio.* How you say? Boyfriend? He *es* in the Florida and I tell him what you doing. He *muy fuerte!*" Lucy flexed one bicep muscle to make her point.

Wayne recalled the conversation he had heard Will have with his father about some AWOL park ranger from Florida who was looking for her.

"Listen, Lucy, I don't want to have any trouble with your boyfriend. Please forget what I said and the wine and everything. Okay?" He stood and smiled nervously. "I just remembered that I have a meeting in the office and need to go now; talk to you later." Wayne scrambled for the door leaving a baffled Lucy alone with Mitsy once again.

At first, Frankie Geyser wasn't sure if he should follow Wayne or try to grab Lucy, but his instincts caused him to do the former to make certain that Wayne wasn't just going to the liquor store for more wine before he returned. *Don't worry Lucy baby, I'll prepare and come back for you tonight.* But the big

Chrysler had difficulty keeping up with the quicker-turning MG, and soon Frankie lost Wayne in traffic. *Go ahead, hot shot. I'll get you another way. It's time to introduce myself to your pal, Hoyle. I'm sure he'd love to learn what you've been up to.*

Will's red roadster wheeled through Bucks County as Wayne drove aimlessly along the tree-lined country roads of Chalfont, Line Lexington, and Hilltown, then farther north through New Britain. When he rumbled past Pearl Buck's historic estate he was so deep in troubled thought that he hadn't noticed the scenery changing as he entered an unknown area. *What am I doing bilking old people and falling in love with an illegal alien whose ranger boyfriend is hunting for her? Will she tell him that I moved on her or will she forget all about it? And what about these old people? Do they know who she is or what they are doing? Mr. Hoover will never become able to review what Will is doing and I'm sure that Will knows that. This situation can only lead to trouble, but how do I tell Will that I need to let him down?*

Private eye Frankie had driven to the law office to see Will Hoyle while Wayne was getting lost in Bucks County. The old colonial looked quiet as the ex-security guard waddled up the handicapped ramp to the front door. He could see Chester Hoover through the window, asleep in a wheel chair, his double chin resting upon his bow tie.

Evelyn was busily typing a letter to Barry Black at Union Penn Savings, and Will was in his office reading a file kept for another of Chet's clients, William J. West. *Man, he must be one loaded old geezer. Once CEO and President of Northern Tile Company, he was awarded twenty-five million as a "golden parachute" in nineteen eighty-eight.* Bill West and Will's grandfather had been close friends, and Chester had written the will.

Evelyn interrupted the silence by buzzing Will upstairs. "A Mr. Francis S. Holmes, private detective, is here to see you, Mr. Hoyle," the secretary announced as she held the Kinko's card far enough away to read without her glasses. "He'd like a minute of your time, he says." Will agreed to meet with him.

"Is your name really, Holmes? Like the famous sleuth of London?"

"Indeed it is, my good fellow" Frankie answered with a bow. "I've been hired, anonymously, to follow and protect the girl, Lucy, and I've come to you because of something I saw today."

"Oh, so you know that I've been taking care of her?"

"I know everything, Mr. Hoyle. I know what you are doing with her and your clients, and I followed your pal and her today. That's why I'm here. Your colleague bought some wine, fed it to Lucy, and had sex with her this afternoon. I watched the whole thing go down, so to speak, at that house where she lives in Oak Park, and she is your responsibility. He is too, right? Well, so you see why I'm here. I think I must report this to my client, but first I thought you'd like a chance to talk me out of doing that."

"We can talk about money later, Mr. Holmes. Where is my colleague now? Do you know?" *If it's true, I have to get rid of him before he screws up everything.*

"He left the girl in a hurry and I lost him in traffic."

Will called Wayne. "Where are you? At Martha's?"

"No, I got a little lost and I'm on my way to the office now;

be there in twenty."

A quarter of an hour later, Wayne Abercrombie was introduced to the private eye sitting across from Will's desk chewing on an unlit cigar. "This is Francis Holmes, the firm's private investigator. How did it go today with Bob Schultz and Lucy?"

Wayne noticed uneasiness in his former roommate's demeanor, but he ignored it and said, "Bob loved her, wants to pay for her college, and buy her a car but Lucy wants a horse." When neither Will nor the P.I. laughed, Wayne became nervous.

"You loved her too and fed her some wine and sausage, didn't you?" Frankie sneered as he leaned into Wayne's face.

Wayne stood up, glared into Frankie's eyes, and shouted,

"Why you no good snoop! You were spying on us, weren't you?"

Will then rose. "Spying is his job, Wayne, and your response just answered his question. Now give me my keys."

"I'm sorry you feel that way, Will, but it's okay because I want out of this sinister practice before it blows up in our faces."

Wayne pulled the keys to Will's car and to the office from his pocket, threw them onto Will's desk, and slammed the door behind him.

Frankie slumped into his chair and said, "Don't you just hate sneaky people like him? But now that he's gone, maybe it won't be necessary for me to report what happened to my employer. But that's up to you now."

"First we need to go check on Lucy to find out if she's okay."

"That's good thinking, but since I'm undercover I'll be waitin' outside, because I don't want her to know I'm watching. I'll follow you."

"Let's talk about money now, Mr. Hoyle, and please call me Frank." The law clerk and the "private eye" had just sat at the bar in Mickey's Tavern, at Geyser's suggestion, after Will had visited with Lucy long enough to be satisfied that she was safe and unharmed. Lucy had appeared content and mentioned nothing about Wayne so Will decided not to inquire about their activities earlier in the day.

"Okay, Frank, but before we do I need to know more about you and why you are investigating Lucy."

"As I mentioned, I have a client who is interested in knowing where the girl goes and who shelters her. I can only assume that there's a bigger fish to catch with her as the bait, but I really don't know who that might be." *Read between the lines, sonny boy; I'm going to find a way to get my revenge on that big-shot father of yours.*

"Listen, Frank, I really don't want trouble for me or for Lucy, *or for dad's run for governor. If someone starts prying, they'll find that I was pilfering the campaign account, and my ass will be arrested.* How much do you want to go away and forget all about it?"

"First, tell me what your pal, Wayne, meant about your practice being 'sinister.' Don't try to bullshit me, because I've been seeing what goes on. What I don't get is your motive. You have a vegetable in your office, sitting in a wheel chair, and you're out visiting all those half-dead people with an illegal alien. Is the girl being forced into turning tricks?"

After his third drink, Will had cast his off his usual cloak of caution and had decided to explain everything.

"Lucy is not a prostitute. I initially had decided to take her with me to see my clients because they're lonely and depressed. Lucy was to soften them up while I sold them on 'updating' their wills. At the same time, I planned to have them sign a living will and a power of attorney that I or the firm can use, as needed, to move their monies around or to put them out of their misery. Think what a total waste it is to have millions of worthless geezers sitting on billions of dollars that could be put to good use. It's been my plan to help change that, and Lucy has proven to be a much greater asset than I had ever imagined. Everyone loves Lucy."

"Now that you bring up the topic, have you been lovin' that hot piece?"

"No. Not that I wouldn't like to."

Frankie sneered. *You lying shyster, I know you have.* "How about your old man, the A.G.; is he getting some action?"

"No. What do you know about my dad?"

"Everything. So, what do you do with the money these old misers dish over?"

Everything? "Charity, mostly, and to help Lucy get her green card and an education. Why do you ask?"

"Oh, I just thought that if there was enough to go around you might funnel some my way."

Will paused, then said at length, "I suppose that something

could be worked out. Tomorrow I'm taking Lucy with me again to visit a really rich old geezer named Bill West. That might prove fruitful, so don't be in a hurry. In addition, your investigation might just get more interesting when Lucy's boyfriend arrives. You might even want to give me a hand in keeping him from finding Lucy if you know what I mean."

"Boyfriend? How the hell could she have one here in the States already?"

"According to my dad, he's some Florida park ranger who she met just after she got off the boat; he has gone AWOL from his post to look for her."

It's that idiot, Whippel. No wonder he didn't pick up. "I know him. His name is Whippel, right?"

"As a matter of fact I believe that it is, but how did you know that?"

"It's my job to know and I'm the best in the business. I'll make you a deal, Willy. How about if I get this jerk out of the picture for you permanently? For a modest fee, of course."

"How about you find him and turn him in to my dad?"

"Whatever you want, boss."

"Five hundred."

"No way! You don't know this dude. He's dangerous and crazy, big as a mountain and armed. I want five grand, in advance."

Will pulled a roll of bills from his pocket.

CHAPTER 26

Martha Kellner took her dinner through a vein in her arm while breathing with help from an oxygen mask. She had responded well. The nurse beside her turned to the tall man standing at the foot of Martha's hospital bed and said, "Sometimes the second time around is better. She seems to be functioning more rapidly than before she had been taken off support. We see this occasionally. When they are given that second chance, so to say, some patients rise to it."

The tall man had been taking notes as nurse Yasaman spoke and checked Martha's vital signs.

"Why did the doctor ask us to call you, detective?"

Bruce Hemmerlein answered, "I'm conducting an investigation into how and why Mrs. Kellner became asphyxiated. I requested the doctors to alert me if there were any new developments with respect to her condition. I was called because Attorney Hoyle ordered the reversal in her care the other day to restore life support. Were you on duty at that time, by any chance?"

"Oh yes, I was, and it was quite the event."

"Really? How so, Nurse Fallah?"

"Well, Mr. Hoyle had a young, Spanish-looking woman with him, she was actually the one who insisted that life support be reinstated. She spoke boldly, with a strong accent, and Mr. Hoyle did what she wanted. At least that's the way it seemed to me."

"The young woman; do you know if she is a relative of Mrs. Kellner?" Bruce Hemmerlein wrinkled his brow awaiting the answer.

"That was the strange part. She acted so sweet and caring toward Martha but didn't resemble her at all. I overheard Mr. Hoyle refer to the woman as Lucy; she had medium dark skin color, with long black hair. Martha is fair with blue eyes and very thin hair. Of course, she could be an in-law or something like that."

The detective placed an index finger against his chin for a moment in thought. He walked to a window, looked outside, and asked, "No flowers?"

"Why, yes, now that you mention it. But loose. Not from a florist in a vase or wrapped. They looked handpicked from a garden."

"Thank you Nurse Yasaman. You've been very helpful. I'll visit the Kellner house in the morning. Maybe her visitor is staying there. In the meantime, if Mrs. Kellner has any other visitors please call me. Here's my card."

"I surely will do that, detective. Good night."

Are you kidding me? This Bright Pointe is supposed to be the top Alzheimer's care place in the state? I'd sure hate to see the worst one. It's elegant enough, but who here knows the difference? Ten grand a month for Persian carpets, a baby grand that no one touches, and a kitchen fit for Rachael Ray with the door locked. There's a perfect rose garden frozen in time; just like the residents.

Will reasoned, during the tour, that the luxury was for the benefit of the families to make them feel less guilty about dumping dear old dad or mom in a *home*.

"So, Ms. Cuzack, as Mr. West's attorney, I'd like to know who signed him into your beautiful facility."

"Mrs. West admitted him and later joined him here. She passed on last year" *I love that; "passed on," as if she just went down the hall.* "It was one of those rare cases where they both contracted the same disease." *Are you kidding! This place is wall-to-wall zombies. If you didn't have dementia before you got here, you sure as hell would before long.*

Will was struck by the irony of the situation: person after person sitting slumped in their chairs, heads down, while surrounded with opulence. He thought that to the patients, it wouldn't have mattered if Bright Pointe were a five-hundred-dollar-a-week flop house.

Ms. Cuzack, Lucy, and Will finally reached the sitting area where Bill West was crouched on a couch before a highly polished cherry coffee table with fresh roses perfectly arranged in a vase. He looked just like the others they had passed on their way. The six-foot-five-inch former high-powered CEO sat with his head down, hands between his knees. He was rocking to and fro in tandem with voices from another time and place.

Their polite and gracious hostess offered them cookies and beverages in the vestibule after their visit and Will asked if she would allow them to meet privately with Mr. West. They would see her later in the vestibule. As the woman walked away, Will positioned Lucy next to his millionaire client and asked her to speak to him in the same way she had spoken to Martha Kellner in the hospital. Lucy sandwiched one of the man's huge meaty hands between both of hers and began telling him her life's story. Before long Bill West raised his head and smiled at his beautiful visitor prompting Will to remove three documents from his briefcase and place them on the coffee table for signing.

Upon their return to Martha's home, Lucy and Will drank Santo Domingo coffee, munching on Bright Pointe cookies. They talked about Bill West, Martha, and Lucy's life in Cuba and earlier in her Dominican homeland. Will called China King for delivery, ordering chow mein for both of them, as Lucy related how she had found El Diablo, who arranged for her seat in the skiff, and how Gomer had saved her from an attacker at Fort Jefferson. She praised Tilly and Will's father for caring about her and thanked Will for taking care of her. Mitsy purred on Lucy's lap until their dinner arrived.

Frankie Geyser, aka Francis Holmes, observed the delivery and exchange at Martha's front door and decided to drive to Mickey's Tavern for another burger and some drinks. He returned after one hour to see Will's car still sitting in Martha's driveway, so he parked again and drank one beer after another from a six-pack as he spied on them through his binoculars. Beer dribbled from the corners of his lips onto his shorts, and the cake crumbs falling from his mouth stuck to the sticky brew with every bite he took. He saw them clearly after Will turned on the ceiling light in the living room. Lucy and Will sat on the couch together and after a few moments the light went out with only a dim glow remaining. Frankie could feel the anger swelling within him as he began to imagine what they were doing.

After dinner, Lucy had cleaned up while Will had gone to his car to retrieve his laptop so they could watch a movie.

"How about 'The Wolf of Wall Street'?" Will had suggested.

"*Es* about real wolf?"

"Yes, Lucy, the worst kind there is."

Will had been able to select Spanish language with English subtitles on his computer and had arranged it on the living room coffee table. Lucy chose the moment when the room went dark to remind him of her love for Gomer and describe her encounter with Wayne. *So nothing really happened between she and Wayne. The P.I. was lying so no wonder Wayne was so upset.* They watched the video in silence. Lucy fell fast asleep.

The weather was changing. A northeasterly wind had arrived, and the sky was rumbling in the distance as private eye Frankie staggered to the house. Geyser belched a foul odor from his beach ball stomach as he walked. A light rain began to fall. Frankie pocketed his revolver to keep it dry as he crouched outside a window and looked inside the living room where he saw them sitting close together on the couch.

The sound of thunder had been getting stronger, and a brief flash of lightning lit up the side of the house and, for a second, its interior as well. Frankie thought he saw Will on top of Lucy, and then Will stood up, next to the couch. He pulled his pistol and crept around the corner just in time to see Will emerge from the house through the front door and jog to his sports car in the driveway. The rain became heavy as he struggled to pull the canvas top over the seats. Frankie sneaked behind Will and aimed his gun. Thunder smacked and lightning flashed just as the ex-security guard pulled the trigger.

Will's body collapsed against the wet car. Frankie opened the passenger door, pushed Will's torso onto the seat, and stuffed his feet and legs under the dash. Frankie saw Will's shoulders slump across the bucket seats as he closed the door before hustling to the protection of Martha's front porch roof.

Lucy, awakened by the sound of thunder, noticed that Will and Mitsy were missing from the living room. She rose from the couch and began calling their names as she searched the first floor. *Mitsy probably hiding from storm and Will maybe go home.* There was knocking at the front door. *Oh, Will maybe locked out.* She hurried to open it and was startled to see Gomer's Sarge, rain-soaked and holding a pistol.

"Well, well, if it isn't the pretty little slut herself? Aren't you happy to see your Uncle Frankie?" He pushed the door wide open and pointed his gun at Lucy, who turned and ran into the kitchen. Frankie followed her saying,

"I don't want to kill you, baby doll. Oh no, I have far better plans than that."

As Lucy struggled to unlock the back door Frankie grabbed her hair from behind and held the barrel of the revolver to Lucy's head.

CHAPTER 27

Her tiny body was shaking as Jeffery placed Miggy on his lap and untied her. They huddled together as they listened to their captors talking on deck. The gas pumps ticked methodically, filling the bellies of the thirsty diesels, as the garbled voices of the crew droned on; to Jeffery, time seemed to be moving with glacier-like velocity. He filled the time by continuing to talk to the child.

"You need to know about this boat, Miggy. It might be useful later. The fuel tanks are located in the stern, the back, on the port side, the left side, of the yacht. Water tanks are filled on the other side to give it ballast or balance. That's important because the boat is very high. It has two helms, places where the captain can drive. One sits high on the flying bridge, and another is in a small cabin with a windshield, like in a car. It was made to be a sport fishing boat, and from the flying bridge the captain can see where schools of fish are swimming. If it's not being used for fishing, the captain usually drives from the helm at deck level. I think that's where The Fish was sitting."

The pumps ceased ticking and the two prisoners listened for the confirming sounds of their captives going to shore. Instead, the mighty engines gunned alive once more. *What's going on? I thought they were stopping for dinner. Why are we moving?* Jeffery watched Migelina's eyes well with moisture as they pleaded with him in silence.

"Don't cry, Miggy, we will get out of this. I promise." he whispered. The child's long ebony hair fell over his shoulder as she buried her face into his chest, her tiny bare feet dangling over his knees. *How vulnerable she is but yet brave. Lucy would love this child.*

Then something unexpected occurred. *Moonglow*'s engines fell silent again and the vessel came to a stop. Gomer had decided that he wouldn't leave Miggy alone another time, so he stood with her in his arms and stepped carefully to the closet. He switched her to one arm, removed the pistol from the closet with his free hand and holstered it in the pocket of his Bermuda shorts. He opened a portal and looked out to watch as Hemingway and Toothless moored the yacht to a weighted ball floating in the water off shore. El Pescado lowered a dingy, and as the three puttered away, the boat circled on its leash in the inter-coastal waterway.

For the first time they were truly alone on the yacht. Migelina remained on Gomer's lap as they spoke in her native tongue.

"I don't want to make you worried, Miggy, but we must take over this boat. I know that you probably are wondering why we don't call the police or swim to shore."

"You don't have a cell phone? You can't swim?"

"Of course I can. All rangers can swim and I do have a cell phone, but it is dead and I don't have my USB cord. I thought about going up to the pilot's helm to use the captain's ship-to-shore radio but it's still light. If Toothless is watching and sees anything, he'll probably kill us. These are dangerous men who can't afford to be caught, and if they think that might happen I'm sure that they would destroy the contraband then kill the animals and us too. We can't let them get away, and I can't leave you here alone. Do you understand?"

"Yes, but I'm scared."

"I am too, Miggy, but we will make a very smart plan together. Before we talk about that, I want to know more about you. How did El Pescado find you and capture you?"

"He is rich and everyone in my city knows who he is. Mami says he pays the *policia* to let him do bad things."

"What kind of things?"

"Mami says he steals rare animals and valuable objects from our country to sell in North America. One day he parked his big car near my cart and went into a house where I was standing in the street selling to people from Canada. Where is Canada?"

"Oh, Canada is a big country north of the United States. It is very beautiful and has high mountains covered with snow. Have you ever seen snow?"

"Only in photographs, but I think I will like snow."

"I promise to have you see some one day, but what happened next with the Fish?"

"Oh, he come out of the house, stopped, and asked me if I wanted to sell all the things in my cart for three hundred dollars. I was happy thinking how proud Mami would be of me to empty the cart and take lots of money home. He pointed to a white van down the street and asked me to follow him there with my cart. When I got there another man, with white hair on his face, opened the back doors of the van and asked me to put everything inside. It was too high for me to reach, so El Pescado helped me climb up and told me that he would hand me the goods to pack inside carefully, so they wouldn't get damaged. Instead he locked me inside."

Jeffery could see fear in the child's face and squeezed her tightly.

"Please continue; it's important for making our plan."

"Inside, another man, with missing teeth, grabbed me and taped my mouth, tied me with straps, and told me that a boa constrictor would eat me if I tried to get away. He pointed to that bag over there on the floor. Then they drove to the boat yard and unloaded everything onto this boat after dark."

"When did this happen, Miggy?"

"I don't remember; it seems like a long time ago but maybe it was only last night. I have been in the dark ever since."

Jeffery gave her a handful of Hershey's Kisses and some of the crackers he had stuffed into his pockets.

"Do you know why the Fish took you and not some other girl?"

"I'm not sure, only I heard them talking while they loaded the boat. El Pescado told the other two that they were not to go near me, because the buyer of me wanted a virgin child."

Jeffery could feel his body tense as he clenched his fists, wanting to make all three toothless.

"Did you understand the meaning of what he had said?"

Miggy lowered her head and softly relied, "Yes." Jeffery stroked her straight black hair with the palm of his hand and asked,

"Did they say anything else that you can remember that might be helpful?"

"El Pescado told the white hairy one that the man who will buy cigars and rum might give him a job. Some other men were going to meet the boat and pay for the crocodiles, and another man in New York was going to buy me and the boa."

"Do you know any of their real names?"

"They were shouting names, but I was too scared to remember any names. What is your name?"

"My name is Jeffery Whippel, but *mi novia*, Lucy, calls me Gomer. Lucy is very beautiful, and I think you will look just like her when you are nineteen."

"If Lucy calls you Gomer, then I will too. Will I meet Lucy some time?"

"Yes, definitely, I promise it, but to get there safely we must plan now. Are you brave enough to help me, or do you want me to take the chance of going up on deck to call for help?"

"I want to help, but I'm scared."

"Of course you are, and I think that the crocs are scared too. Since the boat has stopped moving they have become restless. Even your boa friend is moving in the sack. I'll tie them all tightly but when the boat is moving the vibrations from the engines keep them calm." Jeffery placed Migelina on the bed cushions while he checked each sack.

"Why did you call the boa my friend, Gomer? Do you have a plan already?"

"You are amazingly smart for your age, Miggy. Yes, I have a plan, and you must have courage. My plan is to trick them one by one. Toothless will be first, because he is supposed to return alone. We'll capture him and later get the other two also, but for the plan to work, the boa must become your helper."

Migelina said nothing, but the terror in her eyes told him to be patient.

CHAPTER 28

The boa displayed the markings he expected - yellowish skin with black splotches. He immediately identified the constrictor as the type found on the Cuban islands. He had nothing with which to measure the reptile, but estimated its length to be about eight feet. He held it by the head with his thumb and index finger just behind its jawbone. His other hand cradled the snake at its midpoint. The boa was motionless as he held it, except for its tongue. Migelina stood on her cushion, as far away from Jeffery as possible.

The captives could hear all the activity on the water through the open portal. Ranger Whippel would look through it every few moments and glance in the direction their captors had motored in the dingy. After assuring Miggy that the boa was harmless, he supported his claim by draping the boa around his neck and releasing its head from his grip. The snake remained docile as it continued to smell with its forked tongue.

"You see, Miggy? It won't hurt me. The only time it bites is when it holds small prey before strangling it."

"Then why is the man with the white beard so afraid of it?"

"Golly, that's what I was hoping. How do you know he's afraid of it?"

"Because when they put me in the back of the van, El Pescado told the bearded one to get in with me and Toothless. He shouted 'Hell no! I hate snakes!' And got in the front with El Pescado."

"What about Toothless? Was he afraid of it too?"

"No. He kept moving it closer to me and told me he'd release the boa if I moved even one inch. He told me that it would strangle me and eat me."

Jeffery removed the snake from his neck and held it in front of him with outstretched arms. "Look. I can put both hands completely around its body. It's not large enough to swallow you. Can you see this?"

"*Si* Gomer. But I'm still afraid," Miggy said, peeking through the fingers of both hands.

"That's okay. If I hold its head again, will you touch its tail? Just a touch with one finger." Jeffery took one end by the head. The other end he held out so Miggy could reach the boa. The snake remained calm. Miggy extended one arm and closed her eyes. Jeffery placed the constrictor's tail into Miggy's hand, saying, "hold it for a count of ten. *Uno, dos, tres, quatro, cinco, seis, siete, ocho, nueve, diez* Great, Miggy! You did it!" She had opened her eyes at the count of *cinco*.

"I thought it would feel slimy, but it didn't. Why doesn't it move?"

"Because it knows that it can't get away. If I put it on the floor, it would crawl somewhere to hide. Would you like to hold it now?"

"No," Miggy said, as she sat down.

"Okay, no problem; you were very brave. Now I'm going to put the boa back into the burlap bag, tie it, and show you how to open it. I'll tie it with a tight bow, like you tie shoes. Then to open it all you have to do is pull one end of the cord." After Jeffery returned the snake to its sack he sat next to Migelina and told her his plan to take over the yacht.

The sun had set, and a pink and yellow sky was reflected in the water as Toothless made his way from the marina. The rubber dinghy slapped over boat wakes as its motor pushed it toward *Moonglow*. Toothless was feeling good. He and Hemingway had eaten at "The Endless Crab," where they smashed crab shells with small wooden mallets and finished off a bottle of coconut rum. Toothless complained about having to return to the boat while the others remain on land but later felt euphoric as he staggered to the dock. As the small craft approached *Moonglow*'s port side, Miggy and Gomer could hear Toothless singing "In a New York State of Mind."

"Okay, Miggy, Toothless is alone. You know what the plan is, right?"

"*Si.*"

They heard the dinghy's soft motor die. Ranger Whippel went to the head in the other cabin fully dressed and armed with the .22 pistol. He entered the toilet once again, but this time he didn't lock the door after closing it. Toothless fumbled with the padlock and stumbled down the stairs into the main cabin. Jeffery listened to hear whether Toothless was coming to him or heading for Miggy's compartment. Either way, he was ready. The drunken sailor bumped into the row of rum crates as he teetered towards Jeffery's bathroom cell. As soon as he touched its handle Jeffery kicked open the head's door, knocking Toothless back into the boxes of Cuban cigars. Jeffery spun Toothless around, pushed his chest against the boxes, and handcuffed him in back. A string of profanities filled the room for a few seconds before the ranger could duct tape his vulgar mouth. Jeffery wrestled his catch into the head, strapped him to the toilet, and tied his feet together. He then locked the door and hurried back to Migelina. She had heard the struggle and was waiting at the connecting door when he opened it. Jeffery took the frail child in his mighty arms and said, "one down and two to go." Migelina kissed him on the cheek and tucked her head under his chin saying, "*te quiero mucho.*" The two mutineers sat together and rehearsed their next plan.

El Pescado and Hemingway had made a night of it, drinking and looking for women. The Fish threw enough money around and finally got lucky. Hemingway had "shot and beered" himself around town with no luck. They met at the dock around mid-night, as planned, expecting to be picked up by Toothless. When their crew mate didn't show, they hired a water taxi to ferry them to *Moonglow*. As the boat approached the yacht, they could see the dingy tied to its stern."

The Fish shouted over the whine of the skiff's engine, "that shit head probably passed out, drunk, and forgot us. I'm going to make him pay for this taxi. Find him and check on the girl. Make sure he didn't get to her, and while you're below also check for fuel or water leaks. I'm going to get some sleep and then get us out of here at the crack of dawn." Hemingway bobbed his head and answered, "Okay, but I ain't checkin' them damned reptiles! I hope they're all dead."

"Hey, stupid, that's a lot of dough you're talking about" Fish shouted back. "Just make sure that they're all in the bags and not loose, because they'll kill each other."

"Oh, shit! I don't even want to think about that." Hemingway belted out.

El Pescado paid the driver. The captain and his first mate went aboard the big cruiser. The Fish immediately climbed the ladder to the flying bridge. When he reached the helm, El Pescado slumped into the thickly padded captain's chair for a few hours of sleep before daybreak.

Hemingway was hoping that he could find Toothless and convince him to check the forward cabin. He called his fellow crewman's name. "Hey, Popeye, where are you?"

So, they call Toothless Popeye. Good name for him. Jeffery could hear everything Hemingway said as the bearded first mate descended into the dimly lighted main cabin. The ranger had tucked himself between two rows of contraband. He was crouched, resting upon one knee and ready to jump.

Hemingway first walked to the head, where Popeye was tied and gagged. He checked that the door was locked. He heard noises coming from inside and assumed that their prisoner was still secure. He wasn't about to open the door without Popeye standing guard. The first mate called out to Popeye again, without a response. Reluctantly, he headed for the connecting door between the yacht's main and forward compartments. Jeffery saw him as he passed the aisle where Jeffery waited. After he passed, Jeffery rose in silence and walked, barefooted, on the carpeted deck behind Hemingway and ducked into the last aisle of boxes. Hemingway pressed his bearded cheek against the door to listen as he reached for its handle. The latch rattled slightly. It was then that Hemingway first noticed a sound coming from inside the forward compartment, a sobbing sound. No, more like crying, he thought. Yes, it was the girl's voice. His immediate thought was that Popeye was assaulting the Cuban kid, and he slowly opened the door to peek. He couldn't see a thing inside the room.

Hemingway sensed someone standing behind him, but before he could turn to look, Jeffery grabbed the door handle with one hand and Hemingway's neck with the other. The park ranger shoved his captor into the compartment. The main cabin's lights shined through the open door. Miggy looked up at the first mate and smiled. Her hand held the end of a corded rope that was attached to a burlap bag.

CHAPTER 29

Oak Park

"Hey, sexy baby, what do you say to us finding a nice dry bed to climb into? Or better yet, how about a nice, hot shower together? I'm wet and cold from being outside with your lover boy." Lucy didn't move or make a sound, feeling the coldness of the gun's steel against her neck. "Don't you want to know what happened to your boyfriend, Will? I'll tell you. He's taking his final ride to nowhere in his fancy sports car." Frankie threw his head back, as he roared in laughter, and Lucy seized the opportunity. She jabbed her elbow into his protruding stomach with all of her strength. Frankie doubled over in agony but didn't drop the gun. Lucy broke from his grasp and darted through the basement doorway, closing and locking the door behind her with the key that Martha had kept hanging from a nail protruding from the concrete wall inside.

After Frankie had regained his composure, he tried

forcing the door open. It was solid oak and he realized that even his bullets wouldn't be capable of penetrating. Placing his head near the doorknob, Frankie tried peeking through the keyhole and said, "You know, baby, there are probably rats and cockroaches in that cellar that will soon come to eat you alive. You should come out and let me do that instead. But don't worry, baby, I'll be right here waiting for you for as long as it takes." *It better not take all night because I've got to be out of here before daybreak.* Frankie slumped into a kitchen chair, placed his gun on the table and stared at the basement door. He heard nothing coming from its other side. Lucy hadn't cried or pled for mercy and there wasn't any indication that she was in fear of her situation. Frankie thought, *what kind of a broad is this anyway?* Before long, his head began bobbing from exhaustion until it eventually rested on the kitchen table.

Frankie's sleep came quickly accompanied by snorts and groans. Soon, the dreaded dreams began again as they had done repeatedly since his exodus from the Arizona highway patrol. He could see them from his patrol car, running across a grazing field, trespassing on a rancher's property, all wearing backpacks with a few women carrying children. He was certain that they were the ones being searched for that day. Frankie drove in pace with the Mexicans, as he shouted through the open window of his cruiser, ordering them to halt. The group ran faster and faster until one young mother and baby collapsed onto the dusty earth. The others never looked back as Frankie parked his vehicle and walked toward the pleading woman, unbuckling his pants as he went.

Lucy could hear Frankie's snoring, snorting and groaning from behind the cellar door but she was suspicious. *He could be faking. That is something he probably would try.* But, Lucy was eager to escape from the dark and the smell of the damp basement. She had been debating with herself concerning the pros and cons of taking the risk of unlocking the door when she heard a sound from its other side. It was a rubbing sound. No, wait, a scratching sound. *Mitsy! It's Mitsy, trying to reach me.*

Lucy realized that if Frankie pretended to be asleep it would be foolish for her to open the door. On the other hand, if he hadn't been pretending, she would have Mitsy. Lucy listened carefully, as she slowly began to turn the key but before the lock clicked open, Mitsy released a forceful "Meow" that aroused Frankie from his nightmare. The private eye crept to the cellar door and waited, hoping that Lucy would try to reach for the feline. When she failed to do so, Frankie grabbed Mitsy, held her and began to scratch her neck as he spoke to his prisoner once again. "Real nice kitty I have in my hands. I don't think you'd want anything bad to happen to it, now would you? How about we make a deal? You get the cat and I get you." A huge, belly laugh spouted from Frankie's mouth. Lucy hadn't understood most of what Frankie had said but she could interpret the phrases and his voice to mean that he was going to use Mitsy as a hostage. She continued to remain silent, waiting for an opportunity to jump at him from behind the door.

"Let me make this real simple. I killed your boyfriend and I'll kill this stupid cat if you don't come out." Frankie grabbed

Mitsy by the fleshy fur on the back of her neck and dangled her over one of the boxes that Lucy and Wayne had brought from the supermarket. Misty cried out as Frankie dropped the feline into the box and folded the top closed.

That prompted Lucy to unlock the basement door and run to Mitsy's aid. Frankie grabbed hold of her arm as she passed by him, restrained her while pressing his gun against her back. "Your cat will be okay as long as you do exactly what I tell you to do. Right now, we need to get far from here while it's still dark." Holding Lucy at gunpoint as he cradled Mitsy's box, the ex-cop marched through the front door and outside. He stopped next to Will's car and said to Lucy, "your lover boy is in there, dead as a doornail. Wanna see?" Lucy was too frightened to try and understand what Frankie was saying and didn't respond. They hurried across the wet front lawn and crossed the street to the rented Chrysler.

Frankie placed Mitsy's box on the roof of the car and opened its trunk. A small light attached to the trunk's lid illuminated the interior from which Frankie removed his police-issued steel handcuffs and placed them on Lucy's wrists. All the while, Frankie continued to threaten his captive, detailing what gruesome things he would to Mitsy if Lucy were to attempt escape. Frankie used one of his muscle shirts from the trunk to gag her by tying it behind her head and then ordered his prisoner to climb into the trunk. Once inside, he tied Lucy's ankles together with another shirt.

Before lowering the trunk's lid, Frankie leaned down close to Lucy's ear and warned, "don't forget, I have the cat with me. If I hear any noise coming from this trunk the cat dies, *comprende?*" Lucy nodded her head. Frankie placed Mitsy and her box on the car's back seat and slid in to drive.

The drive to the motel, that seemed like an eternity to Lucy, actually only took fifteen minutes but it gave Lucy time to think. *Poor Will. What happened to him? Did this guy really kill Will? Where is he taking me? Will he kill Mitsy and me? I need to escape, save Mitsy and go to the police, but if he is police maybe they won't help us.* The car stopped and she heard a door open. Lucy thought that Frankie would come for her but, instead, Geyser took the box from the back seat and she could hear Mitsy meowing. Then she heard him walk behind the car and say, "I'm going in to get some rest and I'm taking the cat with me. I'm leaving you here so I don't have to watch you every minute. Don't forget, if you try to get away the cat dies." He had parked the rental in the farthest corner of the motel's parking lot to be as out of sight and sound as possible.

After entering the motel room, Frankie placed Mitsy and her box in a closet, took a hot shower and decided to take a short nap before dragging Lucy to the double bed for sex. A few hours later, Frankie was awakened by the sound of traffic from the turnpike outside his window through which the sun's rays came, lighting up his room.

Lieutenant Bruce Hemmerlein arrived at Martha Kellner's home shortly after sunrise to find Will in his red sports car that was still sitting in the driveway. Not knowing what he might encounter inside Martha's house, the detective called for back-up for himself after calling for an ambulance for Will.

Within minutes of his call, a patrol car with two police officers arrived, followed by a rescue unit. A sergeant accompanied the lieutenant to investigate the grounds and the inside of the home. Once inside Martha's residence, they called out loudly for anyone to answer as they began stalking an imaginary foe throughout the house but found no one. Detective Hemmerlein was examining items on the dining room table when the sergeant summoned him from the basement. "Look, Bruce, there is writing carved into the basement wall at the top of the stairs leading to the cellar. It looks fresh and it's in Spanish."

The lieutenant copied the writing into his pocket notebook and returned to his unmarked police car and opened his computer containing language translation application software. He entered the Spanish words found on the basement wall; "I am Lucy. Will is shot. Sarge took Mitsy and me. Help us!"

CHAPTER 30

Will laid comatose in the intensive care unit of the hospital as detective Hemmerlein worked tirelessly to find his attacker. Following a lengthy investigation at Martha' home, he called Evelyn Carter at the offices of Hoyle, Hoover and Hoyle. She agreed to contact Will's family and employees of the firm requesting them to call the detective at his personal cell phone number any time of the day or night. Evelyn was successful in reaching Will's father and Wayne Abercrombie that morning.

Immediately upon receiving Evelyn's call, Winston Hoyle telephoned the hospital and spoke with the physician's assistant assigned to his son. Having been briefed on Will's condition, Winner requested that his plane be prepared for flight and then called Tilly at Fort Jefferson. Following their conversation, Tilly began packing for passage on the next boat to Key West.

During his ride to the airport, Winner entered the phone number given to him by Evelyn and called detective

Hemmerlein. Winner and Bruce had been grade school friends and it was difficult for the detective to relate the facts surrounding Will's shooting to Winner.

"Sorry to have to talk about this, Winner, but we're trying to find the shooter as quickly as possible." As attorney general, Winner was well aware that the trail in such cases usually became stale after forty-eight hours.

"It appears that there may have been an emotional relationship between Will and the girl who was kidnapped. Can you shed any light on that as a theory?"

"I don't know for sure, but I would guess that they were only friends."

"Is there anyone who would be jealous of that friendship or find it offensive?"

"I can't think of anyone who would be jealous and I don't know what you mean by 'offensive'."

"What I mean by that is that, according to my information, the girl may be an immigrant of color."

"No, I really can't think of anyone I know who would have those feelings."

"Do you know this young woman?"

"Yes. I met Lucy at Fort Jefferson where my girlfriend works as a tour guide and I arranged for Will to represent Lucy and care for her. You see, she entered the United States from Cuba without documentation or even clothing to wear and needs help. Will was working on getting her immigrant status resolved and, in the mean time, thought it would be good for her to have a place to live. That's why she was at Martha

Kellner's house. Martha is a long-time client of our firm."

"So, where were you yesterday and last night?"

"You're kidding, right Bruce?"

"No. I need to ask."

"I was here in Harrisburg all day attending press conferences in front of the capitol. Last night I had a speaking engagement after which I went to my apartment, did some work on the computer, and then went to bed. Now, if you don't mind, my plane is ready for me to board. I'm going to see my son and you'll be able to find me at the hospital."

"Okay, Winner, just two more questions. Do you know of anyone else who knows what you've just told me about Lucy? Secondly, do you know anyone named Mitsy?"

"There are two people who come to mind. One is a guy Lucy knew who worked as a park ranger at Fort Jeff, named Jeffery Whippel. He doesn't know everything I've told you but I mention him because he went AWOL from his post and may be looking for Lucy right now. The other is Will's friend and fellow law clerk, Wayne Abercrombie. They work together so I'm sure Wayne knows all about Lucy. Oh and, of course, my girlfriend Tilly Jewsel who will be arriving here in a couple of days from Florida. I don't know anyone named Mitsy."

Hemmerlein had assumed that the girl who had visited Martha Kellner in the hospital was the missing person for whom they were searching. Winner had affirmed that assumption by referring to her by the same name as nurse Fallah had mentioned, Lucy. "Okay, Winner, and thanks. We'll talk more when you get here." The detective could hear the whine of the Citation's engines as the attorney general boarded for takeoff.

During the next twenty-four hours, Martha Kellner's condition, since going back on life support due to Lucy's insistence, continued to improve. The intravenous feedings, blood transfusions, and oxygen infusion seemed to be having a far better effect the second time around. It was as if Martha had been given a new chance at living. Her attending physician remarked, "It appears that somehow she has found the will to live again."

Chester Hoover's condition hadn't changed. Evelyn wanted to drive to the hospital to see Will but she couldn't leave Chester alone in the office sitting in his wheelchair. She had called Chester's daughter, with whom he lived, at her work place and the daughter promised to stay with Chester during her lunch break. But, the loyal secretary's heart was aching to be by Will's side. She began to cry as she thought about Will lying in the hospital, dying. She remembered him as a young boy, playing in the office while his grandfather and Chester Hoover practiced law. He had been the son she never had. The one that she had lost during childbirth so may years ago. Her voice quivered in pain and her body shook with grief. Chester looked her way and opened his mouth. At first he made a grunting sound, then a shout unexpectedly bellowed forth. Evelyn stopped crying and looked at him in amazement. Her eyes welled once again as she went to him. Chester's head suddenly jutted forward as he forced himself to speak…"Go to Will."

Evelyn couldn't believe that Chester had spoken let alone what he had said. She stood, leaned toward him and bent close to look into his eyes. His lips were quivering and he was weeping. "You love Will too, don't you?" Chester nodded once. "Okay, we'll go together right now." The secretary wheeled her sickly boss down the ramp to her car parked at the curb in front of the offices of Hoyle, Hoover and Hoyle.

They all gathered around Will's bed. His father, Evelyn, Chester and Wayne were all by his side together. Tilly was still in transit. Detective, Bruce Hemmerlein, entered the crowded hospital room and introduced himself to Wayne who was the only person present that he hadn't met. Taking Wayne aside, the lieutenant said, "I understand that you and Will are close friends."

"Yes, we were roommates and fraternity brothers at Villanova."

"I also understand that one of your jobs at the firm was to chaperone someone named Lucy. Is that right?"

"Yes. Will asked me to help her with everyday things such as shopping and learning English."

"Did you see her last night?"

"No, I went home early."

"Well, if she was in your care why was she with Will last night?"

"Will and I had an argument yesterday because he thought I was hitting on Lucy."

"Were you?" Hemmerlein inched closer to Wayne with each question and answer.

"I tried but she told me about her boyfriend from Florida and explained how much she loved him, so I backed off."

"Do you know who or where this boyfriend is at the present time?"

"All I know is that he was some kind of ranger or something at Fort Jefferson when she was there and Will's father told us that he's coming to find her."

"Do you know anyone named Mitsy?"

Wayne smiled and replied, "Mitsy is Martha Kellner's pet cat."

Bruce and Winner exchanged a glance.

"Did Lucy tell you that the park ranger was coming or that she had spoken to him recently?"

"No. She said only that she loved him for saving her life."

"Did she happen to mention his rank or refer to him as 'sergeant' by any chance?"

"Not that I recall. All that I know is that I didn't want to get in the middle of all that. I didn't want to get the shit beaten out of me by that guy."

"So you were afraid?"

"Yes."

Will was still unresponsive when Tilly arrived hours later. She found Winner, the only remaining visitor, holding his son's hand and telling him a story. She listened for a few moments without Winner knowing she was present. He was relating the tale of Mark Twain's, "Tom Sawyer"; the part where Tom cons his friends into whitewashing the picket fence. Winner told her later that it had been Will's favorite bedtime read when he was a child. Tilly cleared her throat and Winner responded by greeting her with a hug.

"Thank you for coming my love."

CHAPTER 31

Migelina pulled the burlap sack's cord, and the boa began fighting its way out. Hemingway looked petrified. Jeffery continued to hold him by the neck as he slapped a wide strip of duct tape over the first mate's mouth and then disarmed him. Miggy scooted past Jeffery and out the door, which she closed behind her. The park ranger tied Hemingway's wrists and ankles then lashed them together, just as a cowboy would lash a calf at the rodeo. Then Jeffery deposited the helpless body on the V-berth cushion, in the same spot where he had found Migelina, leaned toward him, and whispered something in his ear.

Miggy was waiting for Gomer in the main cabin when he emerged from the front compartment, and she was giggling. Ranger Whippel locked the connecting door, scooped Miggy off the floor, and held her as if she were a baby.

"And what's so funny?" It was wonderful to watch her laugh.

"He was as scared as I had been. He looked so funny it made me laugh. What did you do with him?"

"I tied him up and put him in the same place they put you. Then I told him that if he moved even one inch, the boa would get him."

Miggy giggled again. Jeffery rejoiced in watching a childlike sparkle return to her eyes. Then he said in Spanish, "Our plan worked perfectly and you are quite the little actress. Do you still have the fishing knife that I gave you?"

"Si Gomer, I strapped it to my leg in its sheath just as you told me. I have the flashlight in my one pocket and the keys in my other."

"Okay, Miggy, now I must go to check on El Pescado. Count slowly to one thousand. If I'm not back by then do what we practiced."

"I'm afraid."

"Don't worry; I know that you can do it," the park ranger assured her as he climbed the steps to the yacht's stern.

Jeffery moved cautiously into the darkness of the deck above. The deck-level helm sat immediately above the main cabin where Migelina waited, and the boat's mooring lights were just bright enough for him to see inside. The Fish wasn't there. After entering he was able to see the cruiser's chrome wheel. A brass bell hung to one side of the wheel, and an empty captain's chair was in front. It had been swiveled to face the door instead of the windshield. At floor level he saw a small teak door that he assumed led to the hatchway that El Pescado had used to go below and check Miggy before the crew went ashore. It led directly into the forward cabin where El Pescado's frightened first mate now lay tied and gagged.

Jeffery slid its latch to the unlocked position, and with his index finger on the pistol's trigger, he walked out on deck to begin ascending the ladder to the flying bridge above. He had never shot anyone and prayed that he wouldn't need to now.

Clear heavy plastic panels enclosed the flying bridge, protecting it from foul weather. The panels were attached to a solid composite roof and floor that were held together by wide zippers. Mooring lights illuminated the interior of the bridge just well enough for the park ranger to see inside as he peeked over the top rung of the ladder. Just then he heard the sound of a zipper opening. Then he felt the cold steel barrel of a pistol pressed against his forehead.

"Drop the gun, Lone Ranger." Jeffery placed his pistol on the floor of the bridge and slid it inside.

"So, you finally came to get me. That was a foolish move. Why did you wait so long? Did you think that I'd be dumb enough to come looking for you down below? Hell, no. I'd have been a sitting duck. You see, I am not stupid like you." *Golly, he really does look like a fish* Jeffery thought as El Pescado crouched to place his face closer.

"Now back down slowly and don't try anything else foolish." Jeffery obeyed, and the Fish followed with his pistol pointed at the top of the young ranger's head.

When they reached the deck, the Fish waved the pistol, showing the park ranger the way through the teak doorway to the lower helm and into the captain's chair.

"Don't move from there and don't try anything stupid if you want to live. Now, tell me what you did with my men."

CHAPTER 32

When Migelina had finished counting, she reluctantly re-entered the forward compartment to face the crocodiles, the boa, and Hemingway. The flashlight showed her the way around the sacks on the floor. She shined it at the body tied on the bed cushion. It stared at her with wild and frightened eyes. Then she used it to search for the snake. The light found the boa hiding at the base of the stairway. It was curled upon itself like a turban. She would have to step over the constrictor to complete her mission. From above, at the top of the steps, she could hear Gomer talking. He spoke in Spanglish, just loudly enough for her to understand.

"Your man Popeye, the toothless one, is locked in the main cabin's head," Jeffery informed the Fish. "The other one is lying just inside there," he pointed to the hatchway where Miggy waited; her heart pounding so hard she worried that El Pescado might hear it.

With his beady eyes trained on Gomer, Fish reached behind his back and pushed open the door. Out of the corner of one eye he saw a body wrapped and tied in a yellow rain slicker. "Is he alive?" He continued to stare at Jeffery with his pistol aimed at the ranger's chest.

Jeffery shouted, "Yes! Just cut the ropes!"

On cue, Migelina sliced through the two ropes holding the rubber raincoat closed. The crocodile burst forward, up one step and onto El Pescado's foot. The Fish jumped and screamed. Jeffery leaped from the chair and grabbed the Fish by the arm; the two struggled to take control of the pistol, with the Fish proving to be stronger than Jeffery had anticipated. Both big men fell to the deck, and the Fish managed to strike Jeffery on the side of his head with the pistol. The crocodile scampered aimlessly trying to find a way out of the small room.

Migelina sidestepped her way along the wall closest to where the men fought. She could see blood dripping down Gomer's left cheek. She became angry and began shouting for them to stop. The men rolled on the deck with El Pescado ending on top of Jeffery. He raised his arm, about to strike Jeffery's head with the gun again, when the blade of a razor-sharp fishing knife sliced the back of his hand. Blood began streaming down El Pescado's arm. He dropped the pistol, crying in pain. Migelina picked it up off the floor and pointed it at the man everyone called the Fish.

The girl had never touched a gun before that night. Standing over him, she held El Pescado's pistol with her right hand and steadied it with her left; her feet were spread apart and arms fully extended. The Fish could see her index finger on the trigger, and the hammer on the six-shooter was cocked. Jeffery had taught her well as they prepared for their takeover of the yacht. Miggy had even remembered to reveal her killer face (teeth clenched, eyes squinting, and lips curled) as Jeffery had jokingly called it.

Fish told Jeffery where to find the first aid kit. It was in a box beneath the helm next to a large ice chest. Inside the box he found rags, towels, rope, charts, an air horn, a roll of duct tape, power cords of all sizes, and an assortment of tools. The park ranger treated his own wounds and the Fish's hand, telling him that stitches would be required as he bandaged it with gauze, tape, and a wrap. Jeffery's injuries were minor; a small cut and a bruise on his cheekbone. Migelina stood guard with the small caliber pistol and her fishing knife.

It was two in the morning when Ranger Whippel ordered the Fish to take the helm, start the engines, and get under way. He asked many questions about their location and destination as he used duct tape to bind Fish's ankles together and strap him into the captain's chair. Then he captured the croc, tied it inside the rubber raincoat, and returned it below with the others.

The yacht's preprogrammed GPS confirmed what Miggy had told him. They were headed to Philadelphia. From there the digital map showed the boat's course continuing on to New York harbor via the Hudson River. It also pinpointed their location and direction. They were cruising at top speed off the coast of Virginia. Their ETA for Philly was six-thirty the following evening. Jeffery knew only that Philadelphia was in

Pennsylvania, but had no idea how far from the city the Hoyles were holding Lucy. It didn't matter. He would find her. Jeffery commanded Miggy to stand guard while he checked their other prisoners and made certain all hatchways were secure. The little girl tossed her long hair over her back and resumed her combat posture while maintaining a safe distance from the helm and the Fish. Jeffery soon returned and they settled in for the long cruise. It began to rain as he placed cushions on the floor and instructed Miggy to take a nap. They would take turns.

From his Key West Coast Guard Auxiliary navigation instruction, Jeffery recalled the red right return rule: a catchy phrase intended to assist neophyte sailors when navigating in the ICW. The channel had buoys and markers, some red, some green, to guide boats by direction and water depth. When returning to port or when moving south, the red markers were always to be to the captain's right - *red right return* - the right side of the craft being its starboard side and the left being its port side. *To port is left and both words have only four letters.*

As they cruised in darkness he noticed that some markers and buoys were lighted, green and red respectively, with the red lights to port side. They were indeed headed north.

Night rolled to day as the sun's glow drew a thin orange line across the horizon. Standing on the outside deck, Jeffery yearned to have Lucy by his side, watching the sunrise yet again. He began to wonder what their fate might be. *Will she still care about me? Has she fallen for the Hoyle boy? Who could blame her if she did? A lawyer from a rich family with an important father;*

what girl wouldn't go for that? But that's not Lucy. She's different; smart and special in every way. Way too smart to stay with someone she didn't love just for fortune and fame. But how will I find her? I will need help, when we get to Philadelphia, and what will happen to Miggy?

Lost in thought, Jeffery didn't notice the yacht's change of direction until he heard the thump. They had hit a marker piling and were about to run aground. He noticed that the marker was red and to starboard. They had turned around, and the boat's bow was pointed south. Jeffery ran into the cabin, where he found the Fish asleep at the wheel. The cruiser had bounced off a red marker and was headed south toward a green one. Jeffery quickly steered the craft back into the channel and checked its controls. *Two chrome throttles and two chrome shifter arms with three gears, forward, neutral and reverse.* He pulled the right shifter arm backward into neutral and the boat began to pivot right, heading out of the channel again toward shallow water. He jerked the same shifter into reverse, and the yacht took a spin to starboard again, its propellers churning mud on the bottom. Jeffery felt a sense of panic buzz his brain as he yanked the port shifter into reverse, which caused the boat to move straight backwards and head for another piling. *Golly! How do I stop this thing?*

The Fish opened his eyes and saw what was happening. He steadied the wheel with his left hand, and grabbing the knobs of both shifters with his right, calmly put the gears in neutral and the throttles to idle. The big yacht glided to a stop. "It doesn't have brakes," said the Fish, as he sneered at Jeffery, "and it's a lot heavier and more powerful than that shitty skiff we saved you from."

Migelina had slept through the entire event, curled up on one of the padded benches on the other side of the cabin. Jeffery walked to her, covered her petite body with a towel and carefully removed the key ring from her pocket.

"Which one of these keys opens the pad lock to the ice chest?" He held the keys in the palm of his hand as Fish searched for the correct one.

The ice chest contained hoagies wrapped in foil, ice cream sandwiches, fruit, a Zip-loc bag containing cooked shrimp, juice, and beer. They ate and drank until they were full.

"So, Lone Ranger, how do you think you're going to pilot this boat into a crowded city harbor and dock it when you can't even maneuver it in open waters? I'm not going to do it just so you can turn me in. You'd better get off at the next marina we come to in Maryland."

Ranger Whippel didn't respond as he tied the smuggler's hands behind his back and folded a towel on the deck for the Fish to use as a pillow.

"Get some sleep now, you're obviously too tired to operate this boat right now." Miggy continued slumbering on the other side of the cabin.

Moonshine, as Jeffery had renamed the yacht, drifted as its engines idled in neutral. The craft was out of the channel with its hull resting on a sand bar when Ranger Whippel took the controls. He shifted both levers into reverse, backed off the sand, then turned to the north and shifted into forward in the middle of the channel. *I think I'm getting the feel of this; green to starboard, red to port.*

The morning sun had begun to blind his view. Jeffery retrieved a pair of Ray-Bans from the dashboard and slipped them on. He had proceeded cautiously at first, but before long the yacht was hydroplaning across the open sounds and great lagoons of the state of Maryland. He powered down in areas displaying the white "No Wake" buoys and raced at full throttle in open, unrestricted waters. His adrenalin level masked the exhaustion of his body from a lack of sleep, but he powered forward, determined to complete his mission. His brain was in overdrive as his mind started to solve the challenges to come. *We are definitely going to need help when we get there. No question, but the ship-to-shore radio has been ripped out, and my cell phone is dead.* He tried powering it again, but the display remained black. Then he remembered the storage compartment. *There were cables inside. Could one fit my phone? Could it be? Please let it be.*

He fumbled between his knees, reaching and searching inside the compartment until he was able to retrieve a bundled mess of cables and wires, thick and thin, black and white, all intertwined like an osprey's nest. His head bobbed up and down as he simultaneously tried to watch the channel and separate the cords. After a ten minute wrestling match he held one in front of his eyes that resembled a USB cable. "Snap." One end clicked into his Apple 4, and then he heard the familiar bleep of his cellular device coming to life as he plugged the other end into a port on *Moonshine*'s dash.

CHAPTER 33

By late morning Ranger Whippel's cell phone had fully charged, and he decided it was time to make contact with the outside world. *Moonglow* had been cruising well all day and Jeffery had acquired complete confidence in his ability to handle the vessel with its valuable cargo aboard. El Pescado was asleep on the cabin's deck and Migelina was stretching. A no wake zone was ahead, and Captain Whippel knew, from the laminated chart on the dash in front of him, that they would be idling slowly for at least the next twenty minutes. *I need to make the calls in private, so there's no chance that the Fish will hear what I'm planning.*

"Miggy, would you like to drive the boat for a little while?" The girl leaped to her feet and went to the helm.

"Oh, *por favor Gomer. Si, mucho!*"

"Come and sit on my lap and I'll show you what to do."

Miggy chose to stand at the wheel where she could better see out the front windshield.

"Place your right hand on those chrome handles."

Migelina learned quickly.

"Now, see those two white objects floating in the water ahead?"

"*Si.*"

"They mean 'go slow'; no wake permitted behind to rock the docked boats. So don't move the throttles. Okay?"

"*Si.*"

He instructed her about every aspect of maneuvering the yacht, telling her to call for him if she had a question or any problem. He remained by her side until he was satisfied that Miggy could steer between the markers and stay on course. Gomer explained the chart briefly and as he was returning it to the dash he felt something on its reverse side. Flipping the laminated map over revealed a white sticker that read PHILLY, pier 5. White box van with black letters, "Fari's Foods." There was another sticker for New York, but he peeled off only the Philly label and stuck it on the handle of his pistol.

Seeing that the Fish was still asleep and secure on the floor, Jeffery informed Miggy that he was going to the outside deck to call for help. They would need someone to meet them and help them dock when they reached Philadelphia that night.

Moonglow crept forward, silently making its way across the quiet Sound as he reluctantly scrolled his phone's contact list until he reached the name, "Sarge". *I know that I probably shouldn't trust Sarge after what he did but he knows where Lucy is. I'll think of some way to keep him from causing trouble for anyone once I'm sure Lucy is safe.*

Frankie Geyser answered after two rings as he sat on the

edge of his motel room bed in his boxers and muscle shirt. "Hey, Whippel, what the hell happened to you? Where are you? I understand that you're out looking for Lucy. Well, look no farther, dummy."

"How is she, Sarge? Is she safe? Let me speak to her."

"Yeah, she's safe, no thanks to you, shit head, but she's not with me right now. I have her tucked away in a motel *in a trunk* out of the reach of those Hoyle bastards." *I even had to kill one for you.*

"Listen, Sarge, I've been through a lot these past few days thanks to you, and I shouldn't be speaking to you because of all that you've put me through, so don't lie to me." Jeffery was surprised to discover that he was no longer intimidated by Sarge.

"So help me God, Whippel, your girl is fine and safe."

"She had better be and with you as you claim or you will regret it. Lucy is the only reason I'm even speaking with you. You are my only way to find her and have this criminal crew arrested."

"Don't worry, Jeffery old buddy, Sarge is here to save the day and give you and Lucy a happy reunion. That's the least that I can do after the way I have acted."

Jeffery reluctantly related the story about being kidnapped by smugglers, telling him every detail of their daring takeover of the yacht. He then explained their plan to complete the voyage and catch the criminals waiting for *Moonglow* to arrive with their contraband.

Geyser listened, fantasizing about what he could get. *I could use some booze, rum, stogies, exotic animals, and a pretty little virgin too; fun and big bucks for Big Daddy Frankie.* He couldn't believe his luck.

"I think they're planning to meet some bad guys there in Philadelphia at a dock called 'Pier 5.' They'll be driving a white box van with the name 'Fari's Foods' painted on it. Can you call the FBI or someone?"

Frankie wrote everything down on a pad resting on his nightstand. "Don't you worry about a thing, good buddy. Have I ever let you down? No, and I won't this time either. I'll have the cops and your girl Lucy waiting for you when you get here. How's that sound, Jeffery?"

"You have let me down in the past so be sure to do the right thing now. We'll also need someone to take care of Migelina. She's Cuban and speaks only Spanish."

"Hey, that's a real pretty name. I'll take care of that personally. Have you told this to anyone else?"

"No, I wanted to speak to you first to find out about Lucy, but now I'll call Tilly, because she's probably worried about me. I didn't tell her I was leaving, and my phone was dead until today."

"Don't do that if you care about Lucy. Tilly's boyfriend will have every cop in the state looking for her, and he'll probably have you taken out on first sight. It'll be all over the media, and the crooks in the van will get scared off. We need to catch them red-handed. Don't alert the Coast Guard either, because they probably have an arrest warrant for Lucy."

"Golly, Sarge, I guess you're right. I only want Lucy and

Miggy to be safe." *If he does have Lucy, I need to humor him.*

"Speaking of being safe, who's going to bring that yacht into Philly Harbor?"

"I will. I've learned and have taught Migelina too. In fact, she's driving right now."

"The little Cuban chick? Man, Whippel, are you crazy? Let me talk to the boat's real captain. I need to get more details about the guys he's supposed to meet, and you need him to dock that thing safely. I'll bullshit him; promise him immunity or something. Let me handle it. First let me get the names straight so I can convince the crooks on this end to trust me. The boat's name is *Moonglow*. The leader, is known as the Fish. There are two other guys with him, one whose name is Popeye. They're bringing the goods from Cuba as ordered. From here they're supposed to go to New York to make a delivery. Is that all you know?"

"Yes, that's all."

"I need more. Give your phone to the Fish."

"Why? I don't think that's a good idea."

"I need details to be able to convince the Fish's thugs to trust me and walk into the trap that the cops will set. We'll never get them otherwise because if they smell a rat they'll split. You need to trust me or you won't stand a chance of saving Lucy when you get here."

Jeffery paused for a moment and then handed the phone to the Fish.

"Hello. Now listen, Fish Man, I'm you're only way out of this mess. You have no choice but to trust me, and don't let on to dumb-dumb there that I'm telling you this. I hate that horse's ass. He tried to kill me and he got me fired from a cake job in Florida. When you get here, I'll knock him off for you if you give me the girl, two boxes of rum, five boxes of cigars, and five grand in cash. Now, if we have a deal just start talking about all the detailed arrangements on this end, names and all, so he'll hear. When you're finished say, 'are you sure I won't be arrested with the others?' That Boy Scout standing over you thinks I'm going to have a posse waiting to save the day and call him a hero. Instead, I'll be cutting a deal with the guys in the white van. Got it?"

"Yes, I understand," the Fish answered and followed with a detailed description of the plans between him and his men including their names. "Are you sure I won't be arrested with the others? If not, then I'll agree to steer my yacht to the safety of Pier 5." El Pescado handed the cell phone back to Gomer.

"So, Sarge, what did you promise him? That he wouldn't be arrested?"

"Yeah, and he has to trust me because he's over a barrel, no other way out for him. But don't worry, if he's still alive after it all comes down I'll let you put the cuffs on him personally."

"You're going to talk to the crooks that are waiting there? Isn't that dangerous? What if they don't believe you?"

"That's why I needed that Fish Man to give me more details. How could I know all that if the Fish didn't send me?"

"Where will Lucy be when all that happens?"

"Safe as a bug in a rug, waiting for you."

CHAPTER 34

There's a word for a trusting dummy like Whippel; "gull" something. So lame that he's easily tricked and manipulated to do all kinds of stupid shit even after I conned him at Fort Jeff into thinking I was his pal. "Gullible," something like that. But this is the final con job for you, old buddy of mine. Frankie placed his phone in the drawer with the Gideon Bible. *I wonder who the hell comes to a motel to read the scriptures.* He was about to get dressed and go for Lucy when the rerun of *Friends* was interrupted on TV for a special message.

"Breaking news this morning here on Channel Six. The son of Pennsylvania's attorney general, Winston Hoyle III, now rumored to be a candidate for governor, was critically wounded last night and his girlfriend kidnapped from her Oak Park home. County Detective Bruce Hemmerlein has informed Channel Six, exclusively, that a manhunt is underway for a former employee of Fort Jefferson National Park who recently migrated here from Florida. Police ask for your help in supplying any information that could lead to the capture and arrest of this man, who is presumed to be armed and dangerous."

Shit. They found him already? Critically wounded, not dead? And how the hell do they know about the girl being nabbed? How the hell do they know I was working at Fort Jeff? Gotta get out of here. I'll go to the dockyards in Philly near Pier 5. There's must be a crappy motel near there where I can hide out with the girl and have some sex.

Frankie hadn't bothered to shower before tumbling into his shorts, grabbing his belongings, bolting through the motel room door, and clomping across the parking lot to his rental. He hadn't even bothered to check Lucy's trunk prison before wheeling the sedan onto the Pennsylvania Turnpike, following the signs to Philadelphia. He just wanted to get as lost as fast as possible in the big city.

Forty-five minutes later Frankie took the last exit off I-76, dumping him onto Paxton Avenue, just before the Walt Whitman Bridge that humped over the oil refineries and the Delaware River to the Garden State. He made a couple of blind turns toward the ports taking him through a warehouse district, where he spotted a blinking neon arrow directing him to the Puss and Boots motel. It was wedged between a car wash and a truck repair shop on Barge Street. *It's perfect for a matinee with my Cuban babe and me. The old Geyser luck hasn't run out yet.*

Frankie parked behind the motel, hidden from view by two high steel fences. He checked in, no questions asked, and crossed over Barge Street to a pizza shop. Two grime-laden mechanics in coveralls coming out laughed at Frankie's clothing. *You grease monkeys wouldn't be laughing if I blew your faces off with the heater in my pocket.*

An exhausted and dehydrated Lucy attacked the Stromboli and the Pepsi after Frankie set her hands and mouth free and took a seat on the bumper, biting into the pizza while still guarding her.

"Mitsy is good?" His captive's first question caught him off guard.

Shit. I forgot that the damned cat was in the closet. "Oh yeah. She's just fine because you've been a good, little girl."

"I like to see Mitsy."

"You'll see her when I'm ready and not before."

"You bad man."

"Hey, count your blessings, baby, and be happy that you're with me. You have no ID and you're illegal, so running from me will only land you in jail. I am the best thing you have going for you. Just remember that if they don't arrest me, they can't arrest you. So we'll just lay low here until the heat's off and make each other real happy in the bed."

Lucy's mind was racing through the possible scenarios for escape while Frankie was jabbering on and she hadn't understood much. The nourishment had restored her strength and so she decided to keep Frankie talking for as long as possible, whether she comprehended or not.

"You killing Will?"

"Oh no, I never intended to. The TV news reported that he's doing just fine in the hospital."

"You killing Mitsy?"

"No. Not yet anyway."

Tilly and Winner watched the midday and second news report, which stated that a person of interest in the Hoyle shooting had been identified: Jeffery Whippel, former boyfriend of the kidnapped girlfriend of Will Hoyle. They theorize that the ex-boyfriend might have shot Hoyle in a jealous rage after finding them together.

"Oh my God, Winner, they think that Jeffery did it! That's impossible! He would never do such a thing! Besides, you said yourself that the authorities checked every mode of air and ground transportation and there was no sign of him. He can't even be anywhere around here."

"I know, Tilly, but while I'm not at liberty to divulge police evidence at this point, I will tell you that Hemmerlein told me that they found a note that Lucy had written on a wall in the house stating that a Sergeant had taken them. When he learned that Jeffery was a ranger who went AWOL to search for Lucy, he put two and two together."

"But Jeffery isn't a Sergeant: he's a rookie and hasn't put in the time. Wait! What exactly did the note say?"

"I believe that it said something like "Taken by Sarge.""

"That's what I thought! Winner, it's the name that Jeffery calls Frankie Geyser. Please hurry and call the cops right away."

Lucy's talking marathon hadn't deterred Frankie and he took pleasure in gagging and tying her again. He had taken room number ten on the end, just around the corner from where he had parked the Chrysler. Keeping Lucy at gunpoint, Geyser first peeked to check for observers; seeing none, he hustled his captive into the motel room and pushed her onto the bed. The aluminum frame squealed from heavy usage as the stained mattress rolled a foot or so over the linoleum on its wooden wheels.

Man, this dump is so dirty you could plant seeds and grow grass. "Now listen to me carefully. I want you to do a striptease for me while I sit on the bed with my pistol in my hand. Hey, that's a pretty good pun, don't you think? Get it? Pistol in my hand and my pistol in my other hand." Frankie laughed loudly at his witticism, but Lucy hadn't understood anything.

CHAPTER 35

Frankie pulled Lucy from the mattress and stood her in front of the mirror hanging over a blond dresser with two missing drawer knobs. He pressed the remote to power up the 26-inch Zenith. *Crap! No batteries. I guess nobody watches TV here.*

Pushing the "on" button beneath the picture screen, Frankie said to Lucy, "When I find some music on this thing I want you to do a striptease for me. Okay? Do you know what that is?

"*Yo no comprende nada.*"

"Well then, allow me to demonstrate." Frankie pulled his sleeveless undershirt over his head and began to wiggle in front of her. Lucy gasped behind the tape on her mouth, not believing what she was seeing. *Mi Padre! He is hairy animal; never mi seeing such hairy man in Cuba or mi home country.*

Frankie's black body hair engulfed his flabby shoulders, chest, and back, sticking to his flesh from the humidity as he gyrated to the local weather report. He stopped to change the station. *Damn! The cheap old woman didn't even put in cable. This relic works on rabbit ears. I should ask for my money back.*

Lucy twisted and turned the knots that bound her to no avail while Frankie had been distracted cursing the TV, thinking that she had to do something to avoid being groped by the ex-cop.

Frankie returned to her wearing only boxers, which he proceeded to slide down, inch by inch, tucking his thumbs inside the elastic waistband at each hip and moving side to side with each short pull on the underwear.

Lucy felt her attitude of hope changing to despair as she began to imagine what would happen next, she being powerless to prevent it. She said a silent prayer as Frankie dropped his drawers to the floor and began removing her clothes. There's *no one here to hear me.* Lucy backed to the wall with both hands still tied behind her back, and began kicking. Frankie grabbed the pistol from the pocket of his Bermuda shorts and threatened her as he twisted its barrel into her belly button. "Nobody will even hear this go off, so cut the shit."

Frankie's free hand felt clammy against her thigh as he slid it up to her hip, then around onto her buttock, forcing her against his sweaty, bulging stomach. He stepped backward toward the bed and fell onto the mattress, taking Lucy on top of him.

"Boy, you are one beautiful piece of ass, baby doll."

Lucy could feel his body beginning to shake with excited passion as he pressed himself hard against her. Then a loud banging erupted against number ten's metal door. Frankie hollered angrily, "Who the hell is it?"

"The manager! Open up!"

Lucy stood by the bed as Frankie rolled off. "Get in the bathroom," he demanded and pointed the way. "And don't make a sound, or Mitsy dies."

He unlatched and opened the door and was about to unleash his fury on the old woman from the check-in office, but she spoke first. "You owe me ten more bucks lover boy. When you checked in you said you were alone. It's ten more for two occupying the room."

"Are you shitting me? This rat trap isn't worth what I've paid already," Frankie's fighting words were interrupted by the local news anchor on the TV.

"News Flash! Police have identified a person of interest as one Jeffery Whippel, in the Hoyle shooting and kidnapping case. There is a cash reward for information about this person."

"Fantastic! You are the luckiest dude around, Geyser! Here old hag, take your ten and go back to watering your plastic flowers." Frankie slammed the door in the manager's face. *This changes everything. Now when Whippel gets here I need to make sure they'll find Lucy with him and arrest them both, that'll give me time to get out of town with my cash from the Fish and some of the goodies on board the boat, including that little virgin child. She'll be a lot easier to deal with than this Lucy broad.*

"You mean to say that this guy Sarge who we've been looking for is not who we thought he was?" Detective Hemmerlein questioned Winner and Tilly with a look of frustration upon his face. "I wish I had known before the press releases went out. It sets us back and gives this perp more time to get away."

"I'm really sorry, Bruce, but I don't know these men as well as Tilly does. She told me when she got here after you and I had spoken. Do your people have any leads at all at this time?"

"Yes, one that we just received an hour ago, but -"

"That's okay, detective," Tilly interjected. "I realize how sensitive that information may be, so I'll visit the ladies' room down the hall while you two lawmen talk."

"Thank you. We'll only be a few minutes. I must get back to the department." As Tilly walked away, Winner turned to Bruce with hope that the information would be important.

"It's not much, Winner, but it's better than nothing. I'm sure you remember the Turnpike Motel that we frequented during our high school days. Well, the owner called the station to report that one of his cleaning people had found a cat in distress, locked in a motel room closet. I've called Will's friend, Mr. Abercrombie, to come in and identify it as the missing Mitsy. If it is one and the same, maybe we can get an ID, or at least some information to go on."

"Would it help if I asked the state police to help out? Commissioner Noonan is a friend, and I'm sure he would be happy to assist, but I don't want to interfere."

"Thanks, Win, but it's probably a little premature for that. I can appreciate how helpless you must feel. I would feel the same way."

"Thanks, Bruce. Will is my only son and my only child."

Within an hour's time, Winner received a call from

Detective Hemmerlein telling him that Wayne had identified Mitsy, now fed and resting well at headquarters, and that the motel staff had been interviewed.

"We found out that one lone male registered under the name 'Francis Holmes' occupied the room where Mitsy was found on the night of the crimes. Surveillance cameras show him exiting his vehicle in the rear parking lot alone and not appearing again until the morning, when he left without checking out. I'd like you and Tilly to take a look at the digital printouts and tell us whether it is this Geyser fellow."

"So, there was no sign of Lucy. Maybe he killed her and dumped her, or maybe he stashed her away somewhere. This creep is the dirt ball of dirt balls."

"You're probably right about him but, ask yourself, why bother with the cat? If he had killed Lucy, why would he be stupid enough to leave the cat to be found? Could it be that he did it on purpose to divert us? That's enough conjecture. Please come here with Tilly so we can deal with facts."

CHAPTER 36

"My daddy always said, There's a time to fish and a time to cut bait." *No more time for fishing. Now I gotta put the bait on the hooks.*

Frankie yanked Lucy from the bathroom, pushed her back onto the bed, tied her ankles together with a pillowcase and used another to lash her hands and feet together, leaving her in a belly flop position on the mattress. He said nothing as he walked out of the motel room door, scooted around the corner to his rental car, gathered some clothes from its back seat, and returned as quickly as his short fat legs could move him. Upon reentry, Frankie observed that Lucy remained hog-tied, but he tightened the knots *just to be sure.*

Well, at least the damned shower is strong. Feels like one of those Tortuga afternoon downpours. I'll just do the three "S's," change, and get the hell out of here before the nosy old bag up front gets suspicious.

Upon walking cheerfully into the room, he found Lucy lying on the floor grasping the knob of the outside door with the toes of both feet.

"Nice try, sweetheart, but you don't have to struggle to get away anymore. I'm going to take you to see your boyfriend, Jeffery. I think I remember you calling him Gomer a couple of times back at Fort Jeff in Tilly's apartment. I called him that too sometimes. Gomer is coming," he whispered in her ear as he dragged her away from the entrance.

Lucy tried to shake away from her naked jailor thinking, *why he say the name of Gomer? He going to kill Gomer too?* She grunted wildly, rolling from side to side on her back until she managed to release herself from Frankie's grip.

"What the hell's the matter, you wild Indian? Didn't you get what I told you? Gomer. Gomer is here later today. *Comprende* crazy girl? I'm taking you to see Gomer, Jeffery Whippel. I was going to let you get cleaned up but not now, not after this crap. Stay there and be a good little immigrant while I get dressed and ready for work."

Lucy rolled and turned her back on Frankie. *He saying Gomer esta aqui? Here in Pennsylvania? He saying mi looking at Gomer today? I no think is possible,* pero, *mi hero come* por mi! Frankie seemed to be in such a good mood that Lucy decided to relax some and see what would happen. She could hear him whistling as he readied himself. *Maybe now mi getting the bee with the miel.* She stayed calm even as she finally heard the 'clack'-'clack' as he walked toward her, wearing hard heels. She glanced at him and a feeling of danger consumed her.

"Hey, don't be scared, baby; it's just my old highway patrolman's uniform. Don't I look handsome in it? You won't understand this, but putting this on gives me the same feeling that Batman must get when he dons his suit and cape - tough as nails and in charge."

Lucy stared at the knee-high, shiny black leather boots, the motorcycle cap perched upon his head, the black gloves, and the gray uniform with a yellow stripe down each leg, colorful patches on its sleeves, and a glossy steel badge pinned to one pocket. A wide belt had a pistol attached to one side, and cuffs on the other side hung below Frankie's abdomen. She nodded in approval and forced a smile, wincing as the tape pinched the corners of her mouth.

"If you promise to be good, I'll remove the tape." He saw her nod again so he gently pulled it until Lucy could speak.

"*Gracias*, Señor Sarge. I being good for you no *molesta mi, si?*"

"Yes, good deal." Frankie freed her legs and helped her to stand, thinking that he'd take it a step at a time. Eventually, he would have to release her completely for Jeffery to see.

"Today mi looking Gomer, *aqui?*"

"Yes, if you be good, I take you to Gomer. But don't forget about Mitsy. I kill the cat if you run away. *Comprende?*"

"*Si, comprende.* Mi no go for you take mi see Gomer and no killing the Mitsy."

"Exactly," Frankie responded as he cautiously untied her wrists and drew his gun upon completion of the task. "Now wash your face and straighten your clothes; your shoes are in the trunk." He played a little game of charades to get the point across, and Lucy began doing precisely what Sarge had demonstrated.

Frankie's cell phone buzzed inside a breast pocket of his uniform shirt. After checking the phone's screen, the ex-cop pointed the revolver at Lucy. "No talk from you," he directed her, pointing to his mouth.

"Hello, Whippel."

"Where are you now?"

"Hi, Sarge. Are you with Lucy now? I'd like to talk to her."

"What's the matter, Jeffery? Don't you trust your buddy?"

"After what happened at Fort Jefferson, I've been rethinking your plan and I'm not sure that I should be taking any chances until I'm sure that Lucy is okay."

Dammit! What a hell of a time for him to start getting skeptical! "Listen, Whippel, Lucy is sleeping right now but I'll call you back when she wakes up, I promise. You didn't tell me your location."

"We are in the Chesapeake Bay headed north toward the C and D Canal, and the GPS indicates that we still have a long way to go. I'm sure we won't make it by six o'clock and probably not until after dark. It was slow going getting past Baltimore, and we had some storms that brought us to a stop for a while."

"Don't worry, Jeffery, I'll babysit the guys waiting in the van at the docks, and Lucy can stay locked safely in my car until you arrive."

"You'll still call me when she wakes? I need to hear her voice."

"Okay, will do buddy. Talk to you in a little while." *Damn! The guys waiting in the van at the docks won't know about the delay because the Fish can't call them. I'll have to tell them myself. In fact, that's another way to prove to them that I'm there on the Fish's orders. He didn't want to risk talking over the phone, so he sent me to tell them personally. Man, Geyser, sometimes I think you're the smartest dude on earth! Now, what do I do about Lucy's chat with Whippel?*

"That's him! That's Frankie Geyser on the tape, Winner, and he's running to a black car in the far corner of the motel's parking lot. Did someone get the license number?" She turned to Detective Hemmerlein for an answer.

"I'm afraid that the camera's scope couldn't reach that far, and that's probably the reason he parked so far from the door of his motel room. He's not dumb."

"Maybe not, but he is a little crazy and mean enough to kill. He proved that to Winner and me in my apartment. Right, Winner?"

Tilly's man spoke slowly, displaying saddened and swollen eyes, yellowed by stress and puffy red from sleep deprivation.

"She's right, Bruce, that guy displayed the type of anger and propensity for violence that we look for when profiling suspects. I wouldn't put anything outside the realm of possibility as far as he's concerned." Winner and Tilly tag-teamed telling the detective the facts surrounding Memorial Day eve at Fort Jefferson National Park.

Tilly began to weep as she sputtered, "Poor Will! And I can't even bring myself to think about what that pervert could be doing to Lucy. Can't something be done fast to get him?"

"We have a plan. In addition to the usual all-points bulletins going out all over the state, we've Facebooked and tweeted all law enforcement: state, federal, airport security, and military police. They all have his photo, name, and a description of the vehicle that has been sent to every rental car agency in the state. Unfortunately, we have neither photos of Lucy Tejada nor any data, due to the manner in which she entered the country."

"I haven't seen a retraction of the press release about Jeffery Whippel, Bruce, and I was wondering when there'll be another broadcasting Geyser's photo as a suspect?"

"Good question, Winner. We held a conference about that and the consensus is that Geyser is too smart, not to mention schooled in police tactics, to appear in public unnecessarily, if at all. He will also be watching the TV for such reports and we don't want to scare him off just in case he's still in Pennsylvania. The first report probably spooked him but if he saw our last report he now thinks that we are looking for Whippel. The longer he believes that we're looking for someone else, the better."

"I must leave it in your hands, Bruce. My only duty right now is to watch over my son. We need to get back to Grandview hospital."

CHAPTER 37

A b o a r d   M o o n g l o w

It was a common misconception, the Fish thought, that a person makes his or her own good fortune (luck). No, that isn't true, he had decided long ago. You can't make the dealer flip winning cards your way. One can't predict when a nail will lodge in the tire and bring the car to a halt at rush hour on the interstate. El Pescado had never believed in luck, as such, to begin with, and the only luck that he had experienced was bad luck. What a person can do, however, is try to eliminate the bad luck when it comes by making the right moves.

"Hey, Lone Ranger, how do I know that you can trust this guy Frankie and why would he want to get involved in the first place? What's in it for him to help you get there or to give me a break? How do you know that he won't just eliminate us and grab everything for himself?" *I really have no other way out than to hope that he actually does flip to us for a piece of the action. He definitely sounds stupid enough to believe that I'd actually pay him.*

My boys at the dock will see that he eventually gets lots of action - on the bottom of the Delaware River.

Jeffery continued to carefully survey the waters before them. "I'm not discussing that with you; just get us there as quickly as possible. How far do we have to go?"

"Reedy Point is the entrance to the Chesapeake and Delaware Canal, the C and D, and it is 51 miles above Baltimore at the top of this crappy bay."

Strong winds had rocked and rolled them almost continuously since entry into the Chesapeake Bay. In comparison to their passage in the ICW, where the sixty-five foot yacht had been dominant, in the Chesapeake the boat had been tossed like a rugby ball from one five-foot wave to another for hours, its mighty diesel engines nearly being rendered impotent.

"How long will it take us to get to the marina in Philadelphia?"

"How the hell would I know in this weather? In the C&D it's about seventeen miles to the breakwaters of the Delaware River. Nobody knows how much commercial traffic will be up the Delaware to Philly, but it's usually heavy this time of day. Why? What's your hurry, Lone Ranger? You afraid that your pal won't wait around that long and you'll be left alone to fight off my boys?"

Jeffery Whippel refused to reply as he knelt on the bench next to Migelina who was feeling nauseated. *Don't worry about me. I have a plan.*

"Here, Miggy, eat this bread. It's important to keep your stomach full even if you don't feel hungry. We'll be in Philadelphia tonight, where we'll be able to shower, go to a nice restaurant with Lucy, and eat anything we want. Then we'll get a fancy hotel room and sleep until noon tomorrow." The frail Cuban girl took his hand and kissed it, saying "*Te quiero, Papi.*"

"*Gracias, Miggy*. Are you able to guard El Pescado while I go check on Hemingway, Toothless, Popeye, and the animals?"

"Si, *Capitan Gomer*" she answered with a wide smile.

The Fish knew that there was little purchase in trying to move against his captors. Even if he got past the girl, the Lone Ranger would be returning soon. *I can't enter another port and take the chance of being boarded by marine police, so my best bet is to dock in Philly as planned and hope that my guys there can handle the situation. Besides, I have my ace-in-the-hole to play when the time comes.*

"Everything is AOK, Miggy. There are sounds of snoring out of Popeye and Hemingway is about to have a nervous breakdown."

"Why do you call Kenny Hemingway?" the Fish asked.

"He looks like the writer."

"Never thought of that but, now that you mention it."

"Never mind about that; just get this yacht going. Can't we go faster?"

"We already have waves crashing over the bow, so what do you think?"

Jeffery had felt the sea wash against his legs when he had ventured out to check things, so he didn't press the issue. Instead, he dug into the first aid kit for Dramamine to give to Miggy, along with some canned fruit.

Frankie Geyser knew he was on a roll of good luck as he eyed a Latino boy crossing in front of the Dodge Charger he had stolen to replace the rented Chrysler. *A black cat crossing your path is bad luck, but a brown Latino is good luck. It's going to be a great day.* He powered down Lucy's passenger window as he called to the kid. "Do you *habla* English?"

"Yes," the boy answered with little trace of an accent.

"I'm assuming that you speak Spanish too, right?"

"*Poco.*"

"How'd you like to make twenty bucks?"

"How?"

"All I need is for you to do a little interpreting for me for a couple of minutes. You can stand right there by her window." Frankie had cuffed Lucy's hands around one thigh and positioned her hands so that it would appear that she was holding her leg. She felt certain that Sarge would shoot her and the boy if she screamed or asked the child for help.

"Sure, if I can."

"It's really short and easy. I need to tell my girlfriend something important and she doesn't understand me sometimes."

"Okay, I'll try."

"First, tell her 'I love you.'"

"*Te amo,*" the boy uttered to Lucy through the open car window.

"Good, young fella. Now, tell her, 'I'm fine and don't worry, just come to me fast.'"

A puzzled expression crossed the boy's face as he shrugged his shoulders and spoke again to Lucy. "*Estoy tan bueno, no preocupa, pero venga aqui pronto.* That's the best I can do. It's not perfect but she understands."

Lucy smiled at the boy as Frankie reached across her lap and handed the boy a twenty. *He is such a sweet child.*

"That's it? Thanks." he said with a smile as he turned and sprinted down the sidewalk.

"Okay now, Lucy baby, I have memorized what the kid said, so no tricks. I'm going to park right here and call your Gomer. What the kid said to you is the only thing you are to say, and then I'll take the phone." He used his hands in dramatic fashion to assist her understanding. "Do you understand?"

"*Si, comprende perfecto.*" Lucy didn't care what the restrictions were; she just desperately needed to hear Gomer's voice.

"Okay, here we go," Geyser said as he tapped the screen of his cell. *It's dialing but there's a lot of static, just what I was counting on.*

"Hello, hello? Sarge, are you there?"

Frankie hesitated for effect before replying.

"Sarge, Sarge, can you hear me?"

"Just barely, good buddy, the reception is really bad here. I'll put Lucy on now, but I don't know how long it will last; here she is."

"*Hola, mi vida, como tu ta mi corazon?*"

"Gomer, *Te amo. Estoy tan bueno, no preocupa, pero venga aqui pronto.*" Sarge pulled the phone back from Lucy's ear, puckered his lips, made a scratching sound against its face, and pressed end.

Frankie giggled as he put the phone on airplane mode, thinking to himself *Wow! He's gotta be the easiest person in the world to fool. I just hope that he's satisfied now that he's spoken to his chick. Okay now, Whippel, come to Big Daddy.*

Lucy smiled as tears streamed over her cheeks, and, for the first time in a long time she felt happy - even hopeful.

CHAPTER 38

Pier Five

William Penn's celebrated Penn's Landing overflowed with fitness activity. Roller blades rumbled around a yoga group, Latino music stretched the colorful tights of the Zumba faithful, and boxers jumped rope humming the theme song from the movie "Rocky" as Frankie and Lucy sat, watching, in rush hour traffic. Frankie played the drums on his steering wheel while his teenaged prisoner's brain rolled a romantic video in which she and Gomer fell asleep, bathed in passionate splendor.

Pier 5 was only four blocks farther south on Delaware Avenue with plenty of parking for marina patrons. Frankie jumped the curb and parked his stolen Charger on the sidewalk, directly in front of the entrance gate to Pier 5, prompting an armed security guard to emerge from the comfort of his guard hut.

"This is private property, sir. I'll have to ask you to move your vehicle."

Frankie Geyser emerged from the car, tightening his cycle cap onto his head, puffing his chest, and adjusting his gun belt.

"I'm here on official business to meet and protect the crew of *Moonglow*. It's arriving tonight. Do you know the boat?"

The guard softened the tone of his voice.

"Everyone here knows *Moonglow*, that's Mr. Benedictine's yacht. Do you know him?"

"Know him? I'm his right-hand man. In fact, I just spoke to him on the phone an hour or so ago. He's tooling up the Chesapeake Bay right now and I'm supposed to meet him at his slip."

"I have strict instructions not to admit anyone inside the dockage area without a personal request from the yacht's owner. If you'd like to call him now I"

"Sorry to interrupt; what's your name?"

"Marzo"

"Hi, Marzo, I'm Frank," he said as they shook hands.

"Mr. Benedictine is having reception problems due to storms rolling through and we were cut off. I'm serving as his voice today. In fact, I'm going to be meeting his men here to help unload the things he has brought from Cuba."

The security guard's expression appeared serious as he asked, "What are their names? The guys that he asked you to meet."

"Skeets and Squirrel."

" Do you know Mr. Benedictine's nickname in Cuba?"

"Would that be the Fish?"

"Okay, you may enter to wait for his arrival. His slip number is six. Through this gate, down the ramp, and turn left on the dock. You can't miss it."

Frankie descended to the floating docks below. The marina had a horseshoe shape, bordered on two sides by old brick factories that had been converted into luxury condominiums. Dozens of large yachts rocked, ever so gently, in their watery cradles, tethered on both sides to wooden walkways that rose and fell with the tide. Slip number six was vacant, waiting for its boat and owner. Frankie removed one glove to feel the engraving on the lid of a teak chest stationed on the dock. *Moonglow*. Owner: Umberto Benedictine, Sicily.

Lucy, content while waiting in the car for Gomer to arrive, observed a white box van pull to the curb directly in front of the Dodge. Two men left the vehicle and approached Marzo, with whom they conversed as colleagues, and looked at Sarge standing on the floating dock behind *Moonglow*'s slip. The men were muscular and wore black overalls with "Fari's Foods" printed across their shoulders.

Frankie Geyser began to perspire even more heavily in his dark uniform when he spotted the Fish's two men and the white van bearing the same name. *Shit! I never thought about the Philly mob! Could it be?*

Marzo admitted the men, who trotted down the ramp to where Frankie was standing behind *Moonglow*'s slip. He observed that each had one hand in a pocket, which caused him to take hold of the grip of his pistol.

"Are you Squirrel and Skeets?"

"Maybe. What's it to you anyway?"

"I work for Mr. Benedictine. He sent me here to check on things, to make sure it's safe for him to come in. He told me that you guys would be here waiting." The one who had lumpy cheeks, leading Frankie to conclude that he was Squirrel, did the talking.

"We don't need no help, and our boss didn't mention nothin' about some cowboy cop bein' here to meet us. He would have said somethin'."

"He couldn't tell you because he lost phone reception in stormy seas; besides, he can't call you. There's something you don't know."

"There ain't nothin' we don't know about our boss, so you better have somethin' good if you don't want to go swimmin' with them high boots you're wearin'." That brought a loud laugh from the one Frankie had pegged as "Skeets."

"The Fish's yacht has been hijacked by some nut, and he's forcing the boss to bring *Moonglow* in to be arrested."

"Holy shit, Skeets! He knows the boss's nickname in Cuba. So what's with the copper's uniform if you're here to help him?"

"It's a diversion; don't you two goons see that?"

Skeets stepped to Frankie and poked something in his pocket into Frankie's ribs. "What did you call us?"

"Take it easy, Skeets," Squirrel cautioned. "We can deal with him after the boss gets here."

"He's right, Skeets; we need to work together on a plan to

save the boat, Fish, and the cargo," Frankie said. "You want to listen to what I have in mind?"

Winston Hoyle III answered his vibrating cell phone while he sat at Will's bedside. "Hello"

"Winner, it's Bruce calling from District Two in Philly. How is Will doing?"

"Still unconscious, but holding his own physically. The question is whether, neurologically speaking, he will recover all of his motor and sensory abilities. Thanks for asking. So what's new in the investigation?"

"A patrol car reported finding a black Chrysler, no tags, abandoned in back of the scrap yard at the foot of the Platt Bridge. Know where I mean?"

"Yes, we pass it every time on our way to I-95 and the airport."

"Okay, well, it's the car Geyser rented in Florida and the hood is still hot, which means that he's now driving something else, probably stolen. Just wanted you to know."

"That means he's still nearby. What could possibly possess him to hang around?"

"He might be wanting to use the girl, Lucy, as bait for ransom money or maybe she is just a part of something bigger he has planned. Everybody is in this now; the state police, F.B.I., and all local PDs. We'll find him."

"I know you will, Bruce. Thank you. I'm not going to be of much help as long as Will remains in this condition, but I sure do appreciate hearing the latest. Best of luck and if you need my office to help in any way please give me a shout."

"Will do, Win; you just take care of that boy of yours."

CHAPTER 39

"Did you boys notice my hot, primer gray Charger parked in front of Marzo's gate?" Frankie thought that he might have actually seen a bulb light above Skeet's thick black hair, which he wore slicked back to his neck.

"Yeah, and who's the Latin chick sittin' shotgun?"

"That, Skeets my boy, is Lucy – the hijacker's woman and our bait to reel him in. After we take care of that hijacker dude, she's all yours. Just get your rest because she'll keep you up all night; I should know."

"That's one fine lookin' babe. Did you get a look at her, Squirrel?"

"I saw her, Skeets, but don't lose concentration the way you did during the Bruno hit. You damned near got us rubbed out for trying to hit on his daughter. Remember?"

Bruno hit? What are these enforcers going to do with me when this is over? I guess I'll have to take them out, or better yet, let Whippel do it for me. "So here's the plan, boys."

"Hey, Squirrel. Can you tell him to stop calling us boys before

I blow his ugly head off?"

"Yeah, yeah; so tell Skeets you're sorry and give us this plan, lawman."

"Okay, uh gentlemen, I'm wearing this scorching hot uniform to make the hijacker think I'm coming on board to arrest Mr. Benedictine, who he knows as the Fish. They both know that you two are waiting here to unload the goods and put them in that van, so you'll have to stay out of sight until I give you a signal. Meanwhile, I will tell the hijacker that we're waiting for the cops to come for *Moonglow*'s crew and cargo and get him to relax with his woman and let his guard down, because I'm sure that he's armed to the hilt. I'll also tell him that I had you two arrested earlier today and I'm going to use your van to transport everything to police headquarters with the help of a couple of undercover cops."

Skeets began shouting angrily, "See, Squirrel, I knew we can't trust this creep. He's got cops comin'."

"Shut up, Skeets!" Squirrel replied. "The two cops are you and I, dummy. Right, lawman?"

"Exactly, Squirrel. The hijacker doesn't know what you guys look like. Just shed the black overalls before you board. That's it. Simple, right?"

Squirrel had a puzzled expression after Frankie spoke and then said, "I have some questions about this plan of yours. First, how do you just happen to have this hijacker dude's girlfriend?" Frankie had anticipated the question.

"Somehow, probably by talking to the hijacker, the Fish found out that his girlfriend was living here in PA. I found out where she was living, knocked off some guy who was hitting on her the other night, kidnapped her, and brought her here."

Skeets flashed a disbelieving grin and asked, "Oh yeah? Then how's come she's just sittin' in the car all quiet and calm? Answer that one."

"Because she knows that I'll kill her boyfriend and her cat if she tries to get away. She also happens to be undocumented. Besides, she really wants to see the that hijacker dude again; probably hung like a horse."

"Second question," interjected Squirrel. "What are the names of the guys crewing for Mr. Benedictine, and how many are there?"

"There are two, besides him, and their names are Kenny and Popeye. Any more questions?"

"Okay, we're in. How do we get ready for this shakedown?" *If he believes me this will be an easy job and we'll take care of him later.*

"Good decision. Okay, partners, back up the van so it's out of sight from this docking area and get rid of those jump suits. The boss knows the plan, and the hijacker thinks I'm a cop coming to arrest the crew and hail him as a hero. When I board *Moonglow* with his girl Lucy, the two of them will be preoccupied as I signal for you to run on board. Remember, don't look threatening, because you're supposed to be cops backing me up, and don't talk to the boss because you're not supposed to know him. Just start unloading everything and I'll take care of the rest. We don't want this hijacker jerk to get suspicious. I'll be talking to him as if I'm on his side, and if we pull this off right, he won't figure out what's going on until we have what we came for."

"So how do we get the boss, Kenny, and Popeye off?"

"I'll take care of that, Squirrel, as soon as I get my cut."

"What's your cut?"

"I get five grand, some loot, and the virgin girl. After I'm paid, I'll take care of Lucy and her boyfriend unless one of you wants her."

"I'll take her!"

"Shut up, Skeets; you wouldn't know what to do with a honey like that! No; we'll take down both of them while they're in the sack. As the boss always says, 'don't leave any witness behind.'"

"Okay, then after that I'll release the crew and we can all go party at that restaurant I saw nearby. I think the name is La Veranda."

"Yeah!" Skeets shouted, "it's the boss's favorite."

Damn, Geyser, you are as lucky as you are good.

For better visibility through the C&D Canal, Gomer permitted the Fish, with one hand cuffed to the helm and his feet bound, to pilot *Moonglow* from the flying bridge. The sky was clearing, and the sun had begun to fade as the yacht pitched over the choppy breakwater to motor the last leg of its journey up the Delaware River. The boat seemed like a dwarf next to the parade of mammoth freighters lumbering up the murky river, like so many glaciers drifting at sea. Gomer felt relieved that he didn't have to control the boat to that point. *Sarge was right. I was crazy to think that I was ready to navigate all this.*

Miggy and Gomer had stood guard on either side of El

Pescado, staring in awe at the mansions, yachts, and restaurants along the way. The little village girl gazed in wonder, pointing at things to port and starboard that she had never seen before. Jeffery cherished her every ooh and aah, thankful that they would soon be together - *Lucy, Miggy, and me.*

"What is that?" Migelina asked the Fish, pointing port side at a long schooner with four masts.

Speaking broken Spanish, the Fish replied, "It's the *Moshulu*, an old sailing ship used for party cruises here on the Delaware. Came from Italy."

Then, pointing to starboard she asked, "What is that big gray ship over there?"

"The U.S.S. New Jersey," Gomer proudly announced, "I saw it on TV when they docked it there on the Camden side of the river in New Jersey." He had been following the charts all day, making sure that the Fish stayed on course and he knew exactly where they were heading. *Moonglow* zigged and zagged, avoiding obstacles and other vessels in the river's channel, as the yacht passed under bridges supporting bumper-to-bumper traffic between Pennsylvania, New Jersey, and Delaware.

Miggy fantasized that everyone in Philadelphia had been awaiting their arrival as she saw a chain reaction of lights illuminate both shores in tandem with the encroaching darkness. Giant cargo cranes, oilrigs, buildings, and marinas were all adorning themselves in light as *Moonglow* cautiously proceeded up the Delaware River to Pier 5.

CHAPTER 40

"I need to call the dock master and my hands need to be free if you expect me to be able to maneuver into the docking area," Fish mumbled solemnly.

"Don't try anything foolish," Jeffery admonished as he unlocked the cuffs and handed his cell phone to Umberto Benedictine, the Fish, who entered his man Marzo's number from memory.

"I'll need my feet free also, Lone Ranger, if you expect me to be able to turn around to see as I'm backing into the slip." Jeffery offered the Fish a skeptical glance before releasing his ankles.

"Pier Five dock master," Marzo said as he answered the hut's phone.

"*Moonglow* requesting assistance in returning to port, Marzo."

"Standby, please for one vessel preparing to depart."

Why so formal? Is Marzo trying to send me a warning? "Roger, Marzo." *I never say 'Roger'; he'll have to pick up on that. Maybe I'm being double-crossed by that guy Frankie.*

Moonglow sat idling a hundred yards down river from the narrow ingress to Pier Five's marina. Benedictine's eyes shifted to the left and then to the right to see Migelina and Jeffery squinting and smiling at a message painted in large letters across the side of the Ben Franklin Bridge: "Welcome to Philadelphia."

The Fish slowly twisted his neck to glance into one corner of the flying bridge. It was still there, the pistol that he had forced Gomer to slide across the deck at gunpoint during their first face-to-face meeting, two days earlier; *a major lapse in memory, Lone Ranger.*

Benedictine didn't want Migelina to become restless, roaming about the flying bridge, while they waited their turn to enter Pier 5 Marina, so he decided to keep her occupied.

"Look in that bag; it's full of flags." Miggy peered into a white sack sitting on the floor, reached inside, and extracted a handful of colorful satin cloth.

"Each one is different. I fly the flag or banner of the country we're visiting. There's a Cuban flag in there somewhere."

The Fish had always considered himself a dual citizen. Conceived in Sicily and born prematurely in the United States, Umberto, at his parents' insistence had spoken Italian in their home and learned the ways of a citizen of the old country. The Palermo town bur-gee, on *Moonglow*'s bow pole, flapped in the wind beneath the Stars and Stripes.

"Hey, Lucy baby, you've been a good girl while I was talking to the Fish's goons." Frankie sat behind the wheel of the Dodge touching Lucy's free knee as he spoke. "I'm going to miss your pretty little chassis but you're going to be replaced by a younger, simpler model." Frankie laughed aloud as the Charger's V-8 rumbled into action. "Hey! Soon you see Gomer" - *your stupid, dead-meat, boyfriend.* As he pulled away, he saw Squirrel and Skeets in the van. Frankie stopped and said, "Your signal will be three honks of the yacht's horn. Three, don't forget, and come running aboard." Skeets threw Lucy a kiss.

After abandoning the stolen vehicle behind a dumpster on the other side of Delaware Avenue, Frankie un-cuffed Lucy, took her by the hand, ran back to Pier 5, and led her down the wooden ramp onto the floating docks.

"Gomer coming to here *ahora?*"

"*Si*, honey bunch, Gomer come *pronto.*" Man. *I'm even starting to pick up some of this Spanglish crap; wonder if my little virgin speaks any English?*

"Why I no looking at the Mitsy?"

"Hey. Forget about that dumb cat, and get ready for Gomer. As soon as that boat leaves the marina they'll be coming in."

The Fish watched a fifty-foot Sea Ray cabin cruiser nose its way into the Delaware from Pier 5 as he snapped *Moonglow*'s chrome shifters into "forward" and proceeded with the diesels at idle. It would have been a tight squeeze for the two yachts to pass each other through the opening, as he had learned from experience, and the docking area inside offered little space for jockeying for position with other yachts. It was also darker inside at night than on the open river.

Lucy watched with nervous excitement as *Moonglow* approached bow first, then as it pivoted one hundred eighty degrees to display its name inscribed on the transom. Navigation lights, red, green, and white, outlined all sixty-five feet of the yacht from bow to stern and port to starboard, and spotlights shone on the deck. At first she could see no one on board, but a moment later an image came into view from high above the deck, and a voice shouted "Lucy *mi amor! Esta aqui, esta aqui!*" Another smaller figure appeared behind Gomer as *Moonglow* crept in reverse, inching ever closer to Slip "6" and to Lucy's happy reunion with her hero.

Umberto Benedictine seized the opportunity. While Jeffery and Miggy strained to see who was waiting for them on the floating dock, the Fish shifted into neutral and retrieved Jeffery's pistol from one corner of the flying bridge, returning to the helm within seconds, undetected. *Now we will see who suffers the consequences.*

"Hey, Lone Ranger, go down and toss the fenders over the sides, in case we bump going into the slip, and ask that Frankie dude to hand you the lines from the dock."

"Keep an eye on him, Miggy, while I get us ready to dock."

"*Tambien.*"

Even though Squirrel and Skeets had moved the box van, it had been visible to their boss from the flying bridge. *Good. My men are here, so I guess they know what's coming down. It's time to turn the tables on the Lone Ranger and his little Tonto.*

Moonglow's diesels finally went to sleep in Slip "6" to the lullaby of the bilge blowers and pumps excreting gas fumes and water from the engine compartment. They were docked. Lucy and her Gomer kissed and embraced like two honeymooners on the threshold of their Hawaiian hacienda. Migelina hugged their thighs as she listened to Lucy weep with joy thinking, *the nightmare is over.*

CHAPTER 41

"Hi there little honey. I'm your Uncle Frankie, and I'm here to take care of you."

Migelina hadn't understood a word that the cop had spoken, but she distrusted him instantly. She kept his knee-high black leather boots in sight all the way up the ladder to the flying bridge where the Fish waited for him - hand in pocket and finger on trigger.

"Mr. Benedictine? I'm Frankie, the one you spoke with on the phone. I'm on your side, but I need to pretend to arrest you. So, place your hands on top of your head, like they do in the movies." The Fish complied. "Now here's the scoop. Your men are waiting for my signal, which is three blasts of the yacht's horn, to come aboard and remove the Philly cargo. The dummy and his two girls think that Squirrel and Skeets are cops coming to take away the contraband as evidence. They'll also take your men with them, release them, and turn the tables on Whippel down there. Where are your men anyway?"

"They're being held below as prisoners. What happens to me?"

"After everything is unloaded, I'm leaving with that sweet little virgin, my money, and some cigars and rum. You and your boys can have the pleasure of dealing with Jeffery and his woman."

"Seems like you have this all planned quite well," *but you're an idiot if you think we're going to let you leave here alive.*

"Perfectly! You could use a guy like me in your organization, don't you think so?"

"Yes. I was just now thinking about what to do with you."

"I knew you'd recognize talent when you see it. Now, here's the rest of the plan. We wait until it's totally dark to sound the signal, so nobody can see what's going on, then knock off that Marzo guy in the hut and cut the lights."

"No need. Marzo is on my payroll and has my back. In fact, I'm surprised that you're still alive. You *must* have a good line of bullshit!"

"I'm the best! I once conned the needles off an Arizona cactus!" Frankie threw back his head in laughter.

"Hey, Sarge, what's going on up there?"

"It's AOK, Whippel. The Fish here made me laugh because he thinks his men are here to save him and his crew. Come on, Captain Crook, down the ladder you go to meet the cops." Frankie held his revolver over El Pescado's head as they descended to the deck below, and Miggy assumed combat position: pistol raised and knife sheathed.

Lucy held Gomer around his waist as she stared in wonder

at the Cuban child, speaking to him in Spanish.

"Where is she learning this? From you?"

"Yes, isn't she terrific?"

"No! She isn't even a teenager yet! Take the gun from her and take charge. Children shouldn't be handling firearms, and I don't trust Sarge. You need to be very cautious."

"Okay, I will, but don't worry, I have everything under control." Jeffery took the pistol from Miggy and held it ready.

Frankie smiled and said,

"Hey, little girl. I understand that you can run this big boat. Is that true?" Lucy interpreted for her.

"*Si.*"

"Then you must know where the horn is, right?"

"*Si.*"

"Go give it three honks for me, okay?"

Miggy looked at Jeffery, who nodded in approval and winked a knowing smile. She knew the secret that they were keeping from the Fish and she knew the plan.

The girl chose the forward, deck level helm, from where she had steered *Moonglow* through the no-wake zones.

The others waited, watching from the boat's stern, as Migelina walked to the yacht's bow and entered the pilot's room above her former prison berth. After sounding three short blasts of *Moonglow*'s long, chrome horns, she moved to the hatchway above the steps leading to the V-berth, Hemingway, the boa and the crocodile bags. Frightened fingers unlatched the door as she prepared to enter. Lucy's words resonated within her, "You can't trust Sarge. You must be very cautious."

Marzo, Squirrel, and Skeets came running, boarded *Moonglow*, displaying guns and badges, with one yelling, "FBI! Drop to the deck, now!"

Sarge leaned toward the Fish and said, "Good acting by your boys."

"They aren't my men; they're Feds. You've been had!" The Fish grabbed Lucy's arm, placing the pistol from the flying bridge against her neck. "Now you drop your weapons or I blow her head off!"

The agents placed their guns on the deck floor.

Frankie pointed at Jeffery saying, "He's the one you're after. Jeffery Whippel, the kidnapper they named on TV today."

The Fish snapped at him, "Shut up, you fool, and go get the Cuban kid. Two hostages are better than one. Then we can get out of here."

Frankie began walking backwards, pistol extended, not noticing the boats silently approaching from port and starboard.

The Fish gave orders to Jeffery. "Okay, Lone Ranger, now go below and release my men, and if they're not up here in five minutes your girl dies."

Jeffery unclipped the Fish's key ring from his belt loop, turned around, and tossed them to one of the agents, saying, "It's their job to arrest them."

"You crazy jackass! You just signed your woman's death warrant!"

Frankie had his pistol ready as he entered the forward helm in search of the Cuban girl. "Where are you, my sweet *chica?* Uncle Frankie's here to take care of you." He heard sobbing sounds coming from behind a small door, the sobs of a child. He opened the hatch and tried to focus into the darkness below. The sobbing continued deep from within. Frankie palmed the wall as he carefully descended the steps. "What's the matter, honey? Come to me now. We have to get off the boat." No response; just more crying. "Where are you? I can't see you." Frankie took two more steps and landed on something soft. He slipped and fell to the deck floor below. Something curled around his boot, slithered up to his thigh and began squeezing. Frankie screamed and began kicking to free himself but that seemed to make the boa tighten its grip then he heard horrible hissing and snapping sounds a few feet away that made him panic, too frightened to move or utter a word. Suddenly a hand touched his head, and a child's voice said, "*Buenos dias.*"

Migelina latched the hatchway door and ran aft to witness the Fish trying pull the trigger on Lucy, and Gomer rendering a blow to the Fish's jaw that dropped him to the deck. As he fell, El Pescado kept trying to fire the pistol click, click. Miggy threw her arms around Lucy yelling, "It worked! It worked!" The small girl released a clenched fist, displaying a handful of bullets.

Jeffery took a glare from Lucy but shrugged. "It seemed like the thing to do at the time."

They all heard someone shouting from the dock's security hut and looked up to see Tilly, Wayne, and a tall man approaching from above.

A Philadelphia Police swat team stormed *Moonglow* by land as Delaware River Port Authority officers boarded from patrol boats. The FBI agents then went below, apprehended Hemingway, Popeye, and Frankie Geyser, and ushered them into waiting ambulances.

Philadelphia Police cuffed and escorted Umberto Benedictine, a/k/a the Fish or El Pescado, "downtown."

Migelina couldn't stop rattling on about how she and Gomer had commandeered *Moonglow*. Her adoring audience of Detective Hemmerlein, Tilly Jewsel, Wayne and Lucy listened as Jeffery interpreted. "And then we tricked Toothless and Hemingway ... he's really afraid of snakes, you know ... and when I found the pistol up there on the fly deck, Gomer motioned for me to take the bullets out, just like he had taught me the day before."

Another glare from Lucy, followed by another shrug of Jeffery's shoulders, after which they each took one of Miggy's hands.

"And after Gomer spoke to you, Lucy, he thought something was – well, fishy." Everyone laughed. "So he called his friend. That's you, right?" Miggy nodded toward Tilly, who responded.

"Yes. I then spoke to Detective Hemmerlein, here, who notified the other law enforcement teams. Attorney General Hoyle still doesn't know about this. I didn't tell him while he's beside his son Will in the hospital."

Lucy gasped. "He no die? Oh, *gracias a Dios!*"

"No. He is clinging to life support as we speak."

CHAPTER 42

Grandview Hospital

He hadn't felt the impact of the bullet to his skull or its penetration into the lower left quadrant of his brain. What followed was visual: a small black dot on a yellow background that came at him fast, like the nose of a locomotive without a headlight. Bam! It hit him and everything went black. Flash! Within seconds the blackness turned to white before the film clips rolled. There were brief videos of things he could identify, but others of which he had retained no recollection. A twisted wheelchair lay on the highway with one wheel spinning. Lydia Dunbar crawled after him, begging for help. Martha desperately gasped for air as a tube pumping oxygen dangled by her bedside. His father called his name from far away. Hundreds of short, silent movies played bombarding his mind, scrambling his thoughts, and playing with his emotions, before the sounds began.

The movies ended as suddenly as they had begun when the

beeping began. Maybe it was not exactly a beep. Maybe more of a bleeping sound, like droplets of water dripping into a cardboard box - *ninety nine, one hundred, one hundred one, one hundred two. A voice in the distance sounded, as if someone were speaking through an old microphone. Listen. Concentrate. What is the woman saying? It's getting louder.* The voice finally overtook the bleeping, but it had seemed as though he had been in a tunnel of garbled sound for hours before understanding any of the words being uttered.

"Porter to the ER for transport. Please."

Hospital. I'm in a hospital. That's the freaking bleep, a monitor. Then another voice, closer.

"In your world of lawyers you are top dog, so to speak, but here I'm in charge."

I know that voice. Serious, arrogant, condescending, and unemotional - Dr. Boston. Yes, and he's talking to me. Thank you for saving my life, doctor!

"Yes, of course you are, and I'm not here to interfere. I only want to know my son's prognosis."

It's Dad! Hello Father. It's me, Will. I'm really sorry for all the wrong I've done and the pain I've caused. Please forgive me.

"Will's prognosis is poor."

Oh no! They can't hear me, I'm okay! I'm okay!

"The resuscitation specialist who brought your son back recorded a stopped heart and a brain that had flat-lined. That's a definition of death, and it is extraordinary that he is still alive, even with the help of life support systems."

I can hear you! Test me again. I'm fine!

"But since I've been sitting here with him, Will has opened his eyes and has been staring at me."

"Not unusual. It doesn't mean that he can hear or see anything. Even if he could, his brain damage is probably too severe for him to process anything. But don't misunderstand me. I'm dedicated to doing everything within my ability to keep your son alive. I don't believe in people playing God, even when they do it with their own lives through those 'living wills' you lawyers like to force upon us. I refer to them as 'dying wills,' because that more closely represents their actual intent. Having said all that, however, in this case I will abide by your decision as to when life support should be discontinued. It's a question of how long you want Will to continue living like this. It just might become the most difficult decision you will make, even if you become governor."

"Given all that's happened, I'm dropping out of the race for governor, but you're right. It's the most difficult decision I can imagine ever having to make."

No, Dad, please! Don't drop out. It's my fault. Please wait. I'm getting better! I'll make it, Dad, I'll show you. I need to tell you how sorry I am for cheating our clients and destroying their very lives. They have as much right to life as we have. I need to tell everyone how strong it is - the will to live.

ABOUT THE AUTHOR

Paul is a practicing attorney in Pennsylvania whose education and experience, in the practice of law, have been both domestic and international, instilling in him exceptional insight into the lives of others.

Following his Bachelor's and Master's work in government and political science, Paul went on to receive a juris doctorate degree in law and a fellowship to the McGill University International Law Institute.

The author's thirty-five years of practicing law began in the United States Department of Justice, Office of the Philadelphia United States Attorney, followed by an extensive private practice with offices in Pennsylvania and New Jersey. The last fifteen years have taken him to Costa Rica, the Dominican Republic, Panama, Peru, Brazil, Argentina, the Middle East, and Europe, where he studied the impact of foreign laws, languages, and cultures upon the United States. Today, Paul works as a full time author and part-time attorney, primarily counseling the elderly.

CPSIA information can be obtained at www.ICGtesting.com
Printed in the USA
BVOW11s1856071215

429630BV00019B/146/P